The Chri~
Knitti.

De-ann Black

Toffee
Apple

Toffee Apple Publishing

Other books in the Sewing, Knitting & Baking book series are:

Book 1 - The Tea Shop.
Book 2 - The Sewing Bee & Afternoon Tea.
Book 3 - The Christmas Knitting Bee.
Book 4 – Champagne Chic Lemonade Money.
Book 5 – The Vintage Sewing & Knitting Bee.

First published 2014

Published by Toffee Apple Publishing 2018

The Christmas Knitting Bee

ISBN: 9781977009234

Toffee
Apple

Toffee Apple Publishing

Also by De-ann Black (Romance, Action/Thrillers & Children's books). See her Amazon Author page or website for further details about her books, screenplays, illustrations, art and fabric designs.
www.De-annBlack.com

Romance:
The Sewing Shop
Heather Park
The Tea Shop by the Sea
The Bookshop by the Seaside
The Sewing Bee
The Quilting Bee
Snow Bells Wedding
Snow Bells Christmas
Summer Sewing Bee
The Chocolatier's Cottage
Christmas Cake Chateau
The Beemaster's Cottage
The Sewing Bee By The Sea
The Flower Hunter's Cottage

The Christmas Knitting Bee
The Sewing Bee & Afternoon Tea
The Vintage Sewing & Knitting Bee
Shed In The City
The Bakery By The Seaside
Champagne Chic Lemonade Money
The Christmas Chocolatier
The Christmas Tea Shop & Bakery
The Vintage Tea Dress Shop In Summer
Oops! I'm The Paparazzi
The Bitch-Proof Suit

Action/Thrillers:
Love Him Forever.
Someone Worse.
Electric Shadows.

The Strife Of Riley.
Shadows Of Murder.

Children's books:
Faeriefied.
Secondhand Spooks.
Poison-Wynd.

Wormhole Wynd.
Science Fashion.
School For Aliens.

Colouring books:
Summer Garden. Spring Garden. Autumn Garden. Sea Dream.
Festive Christmas. Christmas Garden. Flower Bee. Wild Garden.
Faerie Garden Spring. Flower Hunter. Stargazer Space. Bee Garden.

Embroidery books:
Floral Nature Embroidery Designs
Scottish Garden Embroidery Designs

Contents

Chapter One

Knitting Bees

The little knitting shop glowed enticingly in the Edinburgh street. Wool and knitting accessories were displayed in the front window along with a sign welcoming people to come in and become part of the knitting bee.

The shop was small but organised to accommodate the customers who regularly turned up on Wednesday evenings to exchange knitting tips and gossip. The owner, Agnes, had told me, or rather warned me, that gossip was high on the list of things to do for anyone who joined them. I didn't have any gossip to exchange with them but I was sure I'd leave with plenty of updates on what was happening in and around the city, perhaps even further than that.

'Come in, Tilsie, and meet the girls.' Agnes scooped me into the hub of the bee, introducing me to the ladies who were already seated and knitting their latest projects. They sat around the shop in any available nook, needles clickety–clacking cheerfully. Others worked with crochet hooks creating hats, one woman was busy with an embroidery hoop, and small quilts were being paper pieced with sheer joy.

Snippets of gossip fluttered in the air, were gasped at for a moment, giggled over and then wisped into nothing more than light–hearted tittle–tattle.

I wasn't there to knit along with the ladies at the bee, though I did enjoy knitting and had bought wool and haberdashery items from Agnes' shop several times. I loved her selection of yarns and patterns. She had a great eye for choosing just the right items, always finding something new and irresistible for those who loved to knit and sew.

She'd phoned and asked me to help her with her marketing.

'I have plans to expand my shop,' she'd said. 'Come along on Wednesday night and I'll explain everything.'

So there I was. She had a late night opening every Wednesday. I lived in Edinburgh and worked from home as a marketing consultant specialising in helping small businesses, especially those involved in crafts. I'd worked in corporate marketing for several years, then

1

having had enough of jumping through their hoops of fire, despite earning good money, I'd left that world behind and set up my little marketing business just before my thirtieth birthday.

In the past two years since I'd become self–employed, I'd made a fair living for myself. I enjoyed being my own boss, answerable to no one, especially my ex–boyfriend who was totally against my idea of giving up my corporate career and winging it on my own. He made sure I was completely on my own by packing his bags and leaving me to it. My decision was difficult at the time. I had loved him, so when he left I took quite a sideswipe. I thought he'd be pleased that I had the ambition to set up my own business. But I guess you never really know anyone, or how they'll react when you go against the grain of what they're comfortable with. He liked having a girlfriend who had a corporate career, similar to his. By scaling down as he saw it, I'd taken some of the shine off myself. So he'd gone in search of the next shiny new woman in his life.

As Agnes introduced me, I was handed a cup of tea in vintage china. A large homemade chocolate biscuit balanced precariously on the edge of the saucer. I was tempted to take a bite out of it to make it fit, but I resisted until the introductions were complete, although the generous coating of dark chocolate and scent of vanilla almost lured me in.

The welcome was warm. I'm terrible at remembering names, but I tried to acknowledge every smile and nod that I received before Agnes swept me over to a wooden chair cushioned with a quilted throw. She sat next to me on a chair that was painted a lovely shade of cherry and leaned close to confide in me.

Agnes was taller than me, trim and in her fifties. Her friend Lisa, a cheerful–looking brunette in her forties, who owned a gift shop, handed Agnes a cup of tea and then left us to natter.

'As I mentioned on the phone,' said Agnes, 'you were recommended to me by a friend of mine, Delphine. She owns the Fairytale Tea Dress Shop in Edinburgh. You did some marketing for her and Hetty last year.'

'Yes,' I said, trying not to laugh. Agnes spoke about Hetty, Delphine's shop mannequin, as if she was a real person. Though I supposed Hetty was quite a character, and I'd included her in the marketing of Delphine's dress shop.

'Delphine said that your rates are very reasonable, and from having had a look at your website, I'd like to hire you to advise me on expanding my knitting shop.'

I glanced around. The shelves were stacked from floor to ceiling with the most gorgeous selection of yarns imaginable. It was the first week in June, but Agnes already had a stock of Christmas–themed knitting patterns and novelty fabrics on display. Buttons, trims and all sorts of knitting, needlework and sewing accessories were stocked on the shelves, and the counter couldn't have held any more items if it tried. Expand? If the shop was capable of taking a deep breath it would've burst at the seams.

Agnes clarified the situation. 'I've been offered the shop next door. I lease this shop from a businessman who owns lots of commercial properties in Scotland. He's easy to deal with. His shop lease rates are very affordable. Maybe you've heard of him? Mr Feingold.'

'Yes, I'm familiar with his idea of making leasing affordable, especially for small businesses. If I didn't work from home and wanted to start up a shop, he'd be the one I'd choose to lease from. He has an excellent reputation.'

'Well, I got a letter saying that the shop next door is up for grabs and giving me first dibs if I want to take it on for a year to see if I can make it work. I'm really tempted, especially as it would only be for one year with the option to extend to further years once the lease was up for renewal.'

'Sounds like a very fair deal.'

'It is. That's the problem. I want to make the leap from a single shop to owning two, but I'm worried about jeopardising my trade. Would I risk eating into my knitting shop profits by paying for two shops? What would I do with the other shop? Obviously, I'd have more room to display my knitting products and buy more items to increase my range of stock, but I'm not sure that it would work. When I mentioned this to a couple of friends, including Delphine, they suggested I get proper marketing advice before making my decision.' She took a sip of tea and then added, 'And there's one more thing you should know. Someone else has their eye on the shop next door and she's a vixen with every intention of becoming my rival.'

'She wants to open a knitting shop next door?'

3

'Worse than that. She wants to have a knitting, sewing and embroidery shop and every other needlecraft she can squeeze into her greedy plan to steal my trade.'

'Are you sure about this?'

'Yes. She even had the cheek to come in here to nosey at my stock. I had to ask her to leave.'

'Is this a long–standing rivalry?'

'Nooo. Julie's new to the scene. She's leeching off her rich daddy and posh boyfriend. Her boyfriend is based in Edinburgh. He's from around here and owns a couple of businesses. Now she wants to have the status of owning a fashionable shop. She's planning on giving it a vintage theme, but she doesn't even knit.'

'Why would she want to open a knitting shop?'

'Because it's fashionable darling,' Agnes said in a hoity–toity voice, imitating her rival.

'More money than sense,' one of the women chipped–in.

'The money's not even hers,' said Lisa. 'She's been mollycoddled all her life. Gets whatever she wants. The shop's a whim but it could do untold damage to Agnes' trade, though that little madam will have us to deal with I can tell you.'

There were mumblings of fighting talk and I tried to calm things down.

'Do you have any plans on how to protect your business if this Julie person does secure the other shop?' I asked Agnes.

Agnes thought for a moment and then said, 'What, like paying someone to make her disappear on a dark, rainy night?'

I nearly choked on the crumbs of my choccie biscuit. 'No, I was thinking more along the lines of better advertising.'

My empty cup was filled with more tea and I was given another biscuit — a shortbread biscuit with lavish white icing and a glacé cherry. I didn't refuse. It had been one of those busy days when I'd been running around the city, organising a couple of small promotional events for clients and then skipped dinner to make it to the meeting with Agnes on time.

'You're looking a bit peaky,' Agnes remarked.

'It's been a hectic time. I've taken on quite a few new clients and everyone wants everything at the same time.'

'I hope you'll consider squeezing my shop into your schedule.'

'I'm sure there's something I can do to help you make the right decision for your business,' I told her.

'Have you any initial thoughts on the matter? Is it a definite no? Or do you think that taking on a second shop is viable?'

'My first instincts are that you should accept the offer of the second lease.' I indicated towards the shelves, brimming with products. 'You could certainly do with the ability to display things better. I know that as a customer of yours myself, I'm happy to browse, and understand that some things are tucked so far up on the shelves that I have to ask you to bring them down so I can see them before buying, but I don't mind. However, there are customers who don't like doing that. They like to browse and feel the texture of the wool, the fabrics and other items. You could be losing out on trade because everything's so squished up on the shelves. Though I have to say the Christmas knits and patterns are very nicely arranged.' A little Santa display doll, several inches tall, peeked out at me from the depths of his knitted grotto. He had a mischievous glint in his eyes but apart from that he was so cute. He was on display along with a softie snowman and a reindeer who were housed in a little quilted cottage.

Agnes's face beamed with enthusiasm. 'I'm delighted with this new range of knits, fabrics and sewing accessories for Christmas. I'm always on the lookout for something lovely for festive sewists. I know it's the summer, but most of my customers start making their Christmas gifts now, particularly if they're knitting jumpers, blankets and tea cosies and making table runners and quilts. Lots of my customers come here on Wednesday nights and we all help each other with things to make for Christmas presents. The ideas spark off each other. Customers work on things like quilts for weeks before the items are ready to be tucked away on top of a wardrobe and hidden as surprise gifts for family and friends.'

'I think I'll be buying some of that new sparkly white wool and the novelty Christmas fabrics before I go. Not sure what I'll make with them, but they're lovely.'

'I have a pattern for a fashionable knitted wrap. It's Christmassy and yet suitable for all year round. The type that's handy to wear if you're going out to a party on a chilly evening. Classy and glam. Or maybe you'd prefer to knit a snowman.'

She held up the snowman pattern and I loved him the moment I saw him. 'I'll definitely knit the snowman.'

Agnes popped the pattern and two balls of the white wool into a bag while I flicked through her new range of fashionable yarns and patterns. I selected two patterns and wool to make an aquamarine cowl and the gorgeous wrap. I hadn't knitted a wrap in ages and was looking forward to making it in shimmering white and silver yarn.

'I know you're often too busy to attend the knitting bee, Tilsie, but drop by when you can and join in with us.' She popped something else in my bag of wool. I wasn't sure what it was but it had a bit of sparkle to it. As she'd done it surreptitiously, I didn't ask and pretended not to notice. 'We all help each other learn more stitches and techniques — not that you need to. You're a capable knitter. A love of knitting is all you need.'

'I enjoy my knitting and sewing. I used to knit at school, the usual stuff — pot holders and squares to sew into a blanket. Then teen and adult life got complicated and I never continued with my knitting or sewing, though every time I saw a pattern or new wool in a shop window I'd wish that I had the time to knit or crochet with it. In the past two years I've tried to make time, so yes, I'll pop into the knitting bee whenever I'm not working.'

Agnes smiled at me. 'Maybe we can find time to help each other?'

I nodded. 'I'll check out some statistics and draw up a marketing plan, just an initial outline, to see if the two shops would work for you.'

Agnes reached under the counter and gave me a printout, as agreed, of her current business situation, monthly profits and best selling items.

I tucked it into my bag. 'I'll read these and get back to you before the weekend, but from what you've told me, I think you should accept Mr Feingold's offer, but hold on until I check out all the information.'

'Thanks, Tilsie. I appreciate your help. Invoice me for the cost of tonight's meeting.'

I shook my head. 'No charge, Agnes. It was just a wee chat. Besides, the tea and biscuits were tasty.'

'Speaking of tasty,' Agnes said glancing out the window, 'look at Stewarton. Isn't he handsome?'

Several women stopped knitting and watched the tall figure of a man walk past the shop. He was in his early thirties, well–dressed in a suit, with dark hair and handsome features that made me wish he'd walked slower so I could have a better look at him.

'We need to think of some excuse to entice him in,' said one of the women. 'We have to lure him away from Julie's wicked clutches.'

The eye candy turned out to be Julie's boyfriend.

'I doubt he's interested in knitting,' said Agnes.

'Or any of us,' another bee member added with a sigh.

'What about Tilsie?' said Agnes. 'She's a wee stunner.'

I laughed. 'More like a wee scunner.'

A ripple of laugher circled the shop.

'If I had a nice figure like yours, Tilsie, and shiny fair hair that behaved itself on balmy evenings like this, I'd make a serious run at him,' one of them remarked. 'In fact, if you had a devious–hearted twin, it would be Julie. Slight build, shoulder–length blonde hair, pale complexion and blue eyes.'

The women nodded, agreeing that I was his type if Julie was anything to go by.

I blushed and shook my head. I knew they were kidding, but still...

When it came to men, my confidence was low, having had more disastrous relationships than triumphs. Sometimes I wondered if I'd ever meet the man who was supposed to be for me, or whether this was wishful thinking, like believing that it would snow on Christmas Day. My love life had more slush than crisp white snow and rain rather than sun, but I lived in hope for brighter times when it came to romance.

'He's looking to see if we've noticed him,' said Agnes.

Everyone, including me, chatted and knitted like busy bees.

We relaxed after he'd walked past, but the Santa tumbled from his grotto and his squeaker gave a disgruntled beep.

Agnes stuffed him back up against his grotto. 'And you behave yourself,' she warned him. 'He's for display only,' she explained to me. 'I got him second–hand. His squeaker doesn't work properly and he's a bit skew–whiff.' She demonstrated how he wouldn't stand or sit without lurching over.

'You should've given him away last year with the knitted Christmas hamper,' said Lisa.

'I thought I had,' said Agnes. 'I was sure I'd wrapped him up with the Christmas pudding, but then I found him hiding in the tinsel when I went to put the decorations away in the New Year. He's a mischievous wee customer.' She jabbed an accusing finger into his belly causing him to emit a half squeak from the depths of his...

Agnes nodded at me. 'Yes, his squeaker noises come from his bum. I tried to sort him out with a crochet hook up his backside but it didn't work. Sometimes he sounds like he's breaking wind.'

'He's delightful,' I said, smiling.

'Do you want him?' Agnes offered.

'No thanks. I've had enough of men who talk out of their backsides to last me for years.'

'Speaking of men and their backsides,' said Agnes, 'here comes Matt.'

A sturdily–built man in his mid–thirties ventured into the shop. He had short brown hair and wore body–hugging, dark blue training bottoms and a fitted T–shirt that enhanced his muscular stature. 'Tsk, tsk, ladies. Eyeing the local totty, eh? And I don't mean me.' The dimples formed on his friendly face as he said this, referring to Stewarton.

'Budge up, girls,' Agnes announced. 'Make room for Matt and his inflated arse.'

All the women pretended to squeeze up and the shop filled with laughter.

Matt put his hands on his hips which didn't look particularly out of proportion to me. I thought he had a strapping build on him. Not bad actually.

'Oh very funny,' said Matt. 'I'll have you know that I've cut back on my heavy squats training to reduce my bahookie and cut down on the cakes and sweeties.' He turned to give us a view of his backside. Although he wasn't lean–hipped, his posterior was firm and he looked like he kept himself fit and strong.

A couple of the women relented. 'His bum's not as inflated as it was,' one of them admitted.

Matt gave his backside a reassuring pat. 'I've lost quite a bit of weight. I'm less of an arse than I used to be.'

We burst out laughing.

'I'm less of a *man* than I used to be,' he corrected himself.

We laughed even more.

'What I mean is...' He gave up trying to backtrack. His explanations were drowned out by our giggling.

'Matt owns the mountaineering shop down the road,' Agnes said to me. 'He's harmless.'

'Useless more like,' one of the women muttered.

'I heard that,' said Matt. 'That insult will cost you a cup of tea and one of those tasty iced biscuits.'

'What about your bum?' Agnes said, pouring him a cuppa and putting a biscuit on a saucer.

'No, just a biscuit for me, thanks Agnes,' he said.

Amid the light–hearted banter I felt that I could help Agnes expand her business and wanted to do whatever I could to secure the shop next door for her. It could work. I could help make it work. Then I saw Stewarton walk past the shop, probably having had a look at the next door property. He glanced in, hearing the laughter, or sensing that he was being watched. No one was looking at him except me. The women were too busy teasing Matt. But I saw him, and for a second he saw me. We looked at each other, and I wasn't sure what I felt. He was really handsome, but his dark brooding looks warned me to beware. My heart had been broken too often to risk taking an interest in a man like him. Besides, he was in love with my devious–hearted twin. They were well–suited. Any man who loved a woman like Julie wasn't one that I wanted to become acquainted with.

The pale grey eyes blinked and then he looked away, got into his executive–style car and drove off.

I hoped that I wouldn't see Stewarton again, but instinct told me that I would. If his girlfriend vied against Agnes over the shop property, he could become a formidable adversary.

'So, is anyone going to introduce me to this lovely young lady?' said Matt.

Agnes made the introductions. 'This is Tilsie. She's maybe going to be helping me with my marketing.'

'There's no maybe about it,' I said, deciding that I would indeed help her, even if it was only to bolster the odds against Julie's rich and powerful business boyfriend from thwarting Agnes' plans for expansion.

I'd dealt with men like him during my corporate life. Men who were ruthless, who didn't care about people and were only interested in making a profit. Perhaps I was prejudging Stewarton unfairly, but I'd always gone on instinct as well as information, and I sensed a harsh edge to Stewarton or untamed quality carefully hidden behind his expensive suit. Either way, he'd be a force to be reckoned with, but so too was a shop full of knitting bee enthusiasts. And my money was on the girls.

Chapter Two

The Tea Shop Quilts

I left the ladies to get on with their knitting and sewing and stepped out into the warm evening. June promised to be a scorcher. A summer breeze drifted over the city, meandering along the historic streets and rising up to the heights of the magnificent skyline. The imposing silhouette of Edinburgh castle, aglow with amber spotlights, shone in the distance alongside the gothic spirals, and thousands of household windows were lit up amid the cityscape.

I put my bag of wool and patterns in my car, then I went over to have a look at the vacant shop.

Agnes came and joined me as I peered through the window. The shelves, counter and a display unit remained even though the premises had been cleared by the previous occupant.

The shop was the same size as Agnes' knitting shop. 'What type of shop was this?' I said. 'The fittings, especially the wooden counter, look like they have a vintage style to them.'

'The shop belonged to Ewan. He built the shelves and customised the counter himself to give it a sort of old–fashioned look. Vintage modern I think he called it. Customers loved it. He's moved further along to bigger premises, but when he heard that there was a possibility that I'd be moving into his old shop he said he'd leave some of the fittings. He's a good sort. He's made a success of his business. He sells home accessories, beautiful items for the living room, kitchen and bedroom.' She pointed to his new shop and I walked the few yards along the street to admire what was on display.

Ewan's shop was closed for the evening but subtle lighting illuminated the stylish quilts, throws, blankets, curtains, table covers and napkins. Soft toys were part of the display — rag dolls and pretty softie dolls that matched the floral prints. He had lots of decorative home accessories such as appliqué cushions, vintage prints, wall decals embellished with flowers, afternoon tea designs and many other lovely things.

'I love shops like this,' I said to Agnes. 'Some of the things are expensive but I'd be tempted to buy quite a few of them. Those quilts and throws are exquisite.' I pictured them on my sofa at home.

The fresh colours and floral designs would give a boost to my drab living room. Since I'd started working from home, my house had become part home and part office with paperwork, a desk and a computer taking over the living room and the bedroom. I kept planning to reorganise things to make the house more homely but never found the time. These quilts could work wonders. The turquoise blue tones mixed with white, soft greens and pastel shades made me want to own them. And I loved the vintage cushions and one of the lamps.

'Ewan scours the country for his stock, though he seems to have a reliable number of suppliers, including me. I've had my quilts, especially the vintage ones like my tea shop quilts, and my knitted tea cosies, sold in his shop. Delphine's fairytale quilts and dolls are popular too. She started making them recently but she's so busy with her tea dress shop that she can only supply them when time allows.'

'I like his bed linen. Very cool and fresh.'

'Bed linen and quilts is something he wants to increase and that's one of the reasons why he's moved along to the larger premises.'

I nodded thoughtfully. Two shops separated Ewan's premises from Agnes' prospective new knitting shop — a cake shop and a shop brimming with kitchen accessories. The rolling pins and mixing bowls gave me the notion to start baking cakes again. If only there were more hours in the day.

I hadn't baked my favourite confetti cake since my ex accused me of baking it as a hint that I wanted him to ask me to marry him. Marriage hadn't been on my mind. I was thinking more about the buttercream cake topping and vanilla sponge with the colourful sprinkles. But it resulted in a bitter argument with him saying that I was devious when in fact I just had a notion for confetti cake and wanted to use up the fresh eggs I had in the fridge.

I wandered back to the little vacant shop and took a good look at it. It had great potential, and ideas on how to market Agnes' business started to cross my mind.

I stepped back to take in the view of the two premises. Each shop had a sizable front window, ideal for displays, and a front door, with the doors being next to each other in the middle. 'Were either of these shops altered before you moved in? They look like they were originally one shop.'

'Yes, my knitting shop and the shop next door used to be one premises, but it was divided up into two small units before I moved in. Mr Feingold says that he's happy to have the partition that separates the two shops taken down so that I can have a doorway through to the second shop. What do you think? Or should I keep the shops separate?'

'One shop would be brilliant. It would be easier for you to deal with the customers if it was all in one. You could keep the other shop door closed and this would let you use the full extent of the window display and the glass door would be part of that. It would be better for serving customers too, having everything under the one roof...' My words drifted off as the ideas started to form.

'What are you thinking? I can see you're thinking something grand,' said Agnes.

'I was just picturing what the shop would look like if each part was set up differently.'

'What? Have another type of shop instead of expanding the knitting?'

'No. The knitting would still be the main product line of your shop. That's what's made you a profit, but the vintage aspect that helped Ewan make enough to expand to a bigger shop is something that you could include. Have your knitting, sewing fabrics and embroidery items spanning across the two premises, but keep the current modern yet traditional theme of the shop you've got, and have the other one vintage. It would be like stepping into two different worlds with the same love of knitting and sewing.'

'I like that idea. I could use the wooden shelving and counter that Ewan made and give the displays an old–fashioned theme. I could include some of my tea shop quilts, my fashion knits and expand my haberdashery.'

'Your customers would still feel comfortable coming into the knitting shop as it is, but they could also step into the shop next door, through the adjoining doorway and see an extended range of products with a vintage and retro vibe to them. It would bring new customers to the shops, which would really be one larger shop, without alienating the customers you already have.'

Agnes smiled at me. 'Delphine was right when she advised me to hire you. You've got some great ideas, along with an understanding of craft businesses and what customers who love knitting and sewing want from a shop.'

I smiled back at her. 'I'll be in touch soon. I want to study the market and the figures you've given me.' I went to walk away but she called out to me before I reached my car. Her words floated hopefully in the warm night air.

'We're going to do this, aren't we?' she said.

'Yes, Agnes. I think we are.'

During the next two days I worked on gathering all the necessary information about expanding this type of business in the shop's location. All indications confirmed that this was a sensible move. Agnes really did need more space to display her knitting and needlework products and the profit she was already making from the single shop unit made it feasible for her to afford paying for the two premises. Mr Feingold had indeed given her the offer of a fair deal. A deal that worked in everyone's favour, including his. The vacant shop would be leased by someone he knew would make a success of it, and it would be easier than putting it out to tender or leasing it to someone like Julie who seemed to want to destroy Agnes' trade rather than help to nurture business in the area.

While I did my research, I couldn't resist checking out Ewan's website. He had an online shop, as did Agnes. I scrolled through the selection of beautiful quilts and bed linen, mentally spending a small fortune and forcing myself not to hit the buy button too often. I bought a cotton duvet cover in turquoise and white. Even the thought of it made me feel cooler as I sat in my living room with the windows open on a particularly hot evening.

Looking at the photograph of Ewan was probably partly to blame for my rise in temperature. His sexy smile was unintentional I was sure. The fabulous aqua blue eyes gazed out at me, drawing me in, making me study the contours of his firm jaw, the smooth cheekbones and straight nose. His features had just the right amount of rugged handsomeness mixed with raw sex appeal.

I clicked on his background details and read how he'd been raised by a mother who was a seamstress and quilter, and a businessman father who'd taught him woodwork and artwork crafts. Although he'd considered becoming a sportsman, involved in outdoor adventure training, his love of crafts, particularly home decor, had led him to owning his own business rather than chasing the wild side of his character.

I sipped my iced tea and blinked out of my thoughts, then I was drawn back to admire the broad shoulders beneath the light blue shirt and the rich, dark, silky hair made me think of all the wickedly delicious things I'd like to do to him given half a chance. Of course, I reminded myself, there was no chance of becoming involved with this exquisite man. I'd have to settle for running my hands along the beautiful texture of his quilts rather than his physique which clearly still bore the lean muscles from his sporting past. I sighed and clicked back to the product page.

There was an option to pick up my purchases from Ewan's shop the following day so I decided to do that rather than have them delivered to my house. I'd phoned Agnes and said I'd pop in to chat to her and planned to collect my new duvet cover, patchwork quilt and the rag doll that I couldn't resist buying. The doll matched my decor. That was my excuse. She was so pretty and I loved dolls like this. I imagined she'd sit on a chair in my living room and look lovely. A little treat for myself.

The afternoon sun highlighted the Edinburgh street in all its glory. Everyone was dressed for the summertime and there was an air of holiday happiness throughout the city. I'd dealt with two other businesses that morning and by mid–day everyone was relishing the heat. A long, cold, rainy winter had overlapped into the spring. Now that it was summer and the sun was out, shoppers were making the most of it and many of them dressed in bright colours and cool fabrics. I was glad I'd worn a lightweight dress in a soft flowery print and comfy pumps. A welcome breeze brushed against my bare legs and wafted through the fabric of my dress as I walked from my car towards Agnes' shop.

In the daylight, the knitting shop looked as appealing as it had all lit up at night. I noticed she'd changed the window display to match the summer season. Blues, sea greens and lemon–coloured yarns filled the front window. It was times like this that I wished I could relax, sit out in my garden in the sunshine and knit a cotton shrug in those bright summery colours.

I stepped inside the shop. 'Your window looks fantastic,' I said to Agnes. Three customers were browsing through the yarns and patterns. Sets of pretty knitted wrist warmers included fairy cake designs and ice cream cones in delicious strawberry, chocolate, mint and vanilla yarns.

'Thanks, Tilsie.' Agnes glanced at the folder I was carrying along with my bag.

'Have you got a moment?' I said.

I opened the folder and we stepped behind the counter while the customers continued browsing. 'I'll leave a copy of the marketing plan that I've made for you. It gives you details of what I envisage the two shops would look like if you presented them as one.'

'So you think I should accept Mr Feingold's offer?' She sounded so hopeful.

'Definitely.'

She gave me a squeeze. 'I'll phone his office this afternoon. Is there anything I should ask him or tell him? Apart from yes I want the other shop and when do I get the keys.'

'Ask him how soon the partition separating the two shops can be taken down. Find out the details and try to get this done as soon as possible. There's bound to be some dust and debris so there's no point in setting up the new displays and then having to clean everything again.'

She scribbled this down. 'Anything else?'

'Yes, ask him if you can change the facia so that the exterior sign can be altered to include both shops and make them one. Mr Feingold is reasonable and he's done things like this for other businesses, or so I've heard, so he'll help sort that out for you.'

'A new sign for the shop. I can't wait.'

While we chatted she served the customers and advised a couple of them on tricky parts of their knitting patterns. One of them was planning to knit tea cosies as the start of her Christmas gift knitting and wasn't sure whether to fluff the yarn on her snowball tea cosy with a teasel brush or make a Christmas tree tea cosy instead.

'Once you've spoken to Mr Feingold and he's confirmed that you can have the lease,' I advised her, 'you should start thinking about items of stock you'll need, especially the Christmas range.'

Agnes nodded. 'I know the day's a scorcher and snowmen and Christmas trees seem months away, but you know that the festive fabrics and yarns do a great trade during the summer when crafters start to make things ready for Christmas.'

16

'I'm hoping to make a start on knitting the snowman.' In truth, I hadn't even peeked inside the bag of wool I'd bought. 'He'll be an ideal partner for my new rag doll. I've bought a doll and some things from Ewan. I ordered them online. Couldn't resist.'

'Fair warning,' she said, giving me a knowing smile, 'Ewan's hard to resist as well. Have you met him?'

'No, but I saw his picture on his website.'

'It doesn't do him justice. He's far more sexy in real life, especially when he's wearing less clothes.'

A couple of the customers overheard and laughed at us.

'I was just warning Tilsie about Ewan,' Agnes said to them. 'He's wearing a white shirt today with the sleeves rolled up and unbuttoned further than usual.'

'Ooh–er,' one of the ladies remarked. 'I'll need to walk past his shop on my way home.'

'You live in the other direction,' Agnes reminded her.

'Ewan's worth the detour,' she said.

We were laughing when Stewarton drove up in his sleek black car. He wore a suit and stepped out into the sun impervious to the heat. The cool grey eyes noticed me watching him through the window of the shop. Again, a connection was made. A moment, a flicker of something...

'He's nice too,' one of the women remarked.

'He belongs to Julie,' said Agnes.

The women nodded, shrugged, and then went back to browsing through the yarns and haberdashery items.

'I'd better tell Stewarton that I'm taking on the lease for the shop,' Agnes said to me. 'That's him having another look at the property.' She hurried outside. I followed her in case she needed back–up.

Stewarton looked round when she announced, 'Tell Julie I'm accepting Mr Feingold's offer to lease this shop, so it's off the market.'

The grey eyes flicked at me. He wasn't happy. About having to tell Julie? Or that Agnes had pipped them to the lease deal? I didn't know. Stewarton's handsome features gave no hint of what his thoughts were.

'Have you signed the agreement?' His tone was confident. Too confident.

'Well...I haven't actually —'

I cut–in, fearing he would try to scupper the deal for her. 'I'm handling Agnes' marketing.' I put as much challenge in my voice as possible and although I barely came up to his shoulders in height, I was quite prepared to contest the issue if he pushed it.

He eyed me carefully. 'Really?'

'Don't let the wee flowery dress fool you,' Agnes told him. 'Tilsie is an expert marketing consultant.'

'Did I imply that she wasn't?' he asked her.

'Yes,' she told him. 'Your tone certainly did.'

I cheered inside. Go Agnes!

He looked away from her and spoke to me. 'Is this true or are you lying so that I won't make Feingold an offer he wouldn't refuse? I've a feeling that the agreement hasn't been signed yet.'

I decided to lie. His attitude and the likelihood that he could make a whopper of an offer to win the lease warranted a fib. 'The agreement has been made.' I hoped the bluntness of my tone would settle any further haggling.

He looked at me again. Right through me. He knew I was lying. He knew.

'I'll tell Julie,' he said to Agnes and then went back to his car and drove off.

We both sighed with relief.

'Thanks for telling porky pies for me,' she said.

'Phone Mr Feingold now before Stewarton or Julie does,' I told her.

Agnes hurried into the shop. 'Keep an eye on the customers for me.'

She didn't give me any chance to refuse.

I was helping two customers choose their Christmas wool to knit festive blankets and a knitted Christmas tree with appliqué baubles when Ewan walked into the shop. I recognised him from his website photo though I wasn't prepared for him to be quite so gorgeous and imposing.

'I wanted a quick word with Agnes,' he said to me. 'Is she busy?'

The face that I'd studied for far too long the previous night gazed down at me. He was as tall as Stewarton and had a sex appeal that I wasn't used to. I'd dealt with all different types of men socially and in business, but few of them had Ewan's looks. I didn't usually wilt when it came to chatting to fine–looking men. I wasn't the giddy type. And often the handsome ones weren't particularly loveable. But my heart rate doubled and I felt myself blush like a giddy teen.

He smiled at me. 'A hot day.' There was no hint that he knew the effect he had on me.

'Yes. Scorching hot.' And I wasn't talking about the weather.

His eyes were more aquamarine than in the photograph. Agnes was right. The photograph on his website didn't do him justice.

'Agnes is making a business call,' I told him. 'She won't be long.'

'I'll come back later.'

I watched him step out into the bright sunshine. The rolled up sleeves of his white shirt accentuated his light golden tanned forearms. He moved like a man who was fit and fast. Although he'd left his sporting life behind him in favour of pursuing his business, I could see the inbuilt strength in him.

'Was that Ewan?' Agnes said, hurrying through from the back of the shop.

'Yes, he wants to have a word with you.'

'You're blushing like a beacon,' she said.

I fanned myself with the knitted reindeer pattern.

'He's a hottie, isn't he?' she said.

Oh. Yes.

'Is he still single?' a customer asked as she put the knitting needles and yarn she wanted to buy down on the counter.

Agnes rang her purchases through the till as she explained about Ewan's ex–girlfriend running off with his cousin which had caused a temporary rift in the family. Apparently the affair didn't last and she'd attempted to get back together again with Ewan.

'Did he take her back?' I said, becoming engrossed in the gossip.

'No,' said Agnes. 'And rightly so. She was stunning, a former model. But he didn't trust her any longer.'

'I heard that he'd been going to ask her to marry him when she chucked him for his cousin, and then realised she'd made a mistake,' said the customer.

Agnes shook her head and popped a sample of a new yarn into the bag along with the knitting needles. 'No, he did love her, but there was no hint of marriage. He dated her for just over a year.' She glanced at me and winked. 'So he's single.'

Chapter Three

Confetti Cake

I felt a little bit nervous as I approached Ewan's shop to pick up the things I'd ordered. I squinted against the sunlight that glinted off the window. The shop door was open and he was serving a customer.

He looked up when he saw me.

Calm down, I told myself. Do not blush and do not act like an idiot.

I browsed around his shop while he wrapped up a couple of cushions and carefully folded one of the quilts that the customer had bought. I was glad that the air felt cooler inside the shop and a light breeze wafted in.

I was momentarily lost in the beautiful fabrics and details of one of Agnes' tea shop quilts. It had little shops, roses, bluebells and bunting in the design along with a beehive and bumblebees. A sewing machine, teapot and pansy print teacup and saucer were incorporated into the quilt pattern. I loved it and wished I could make a quilt like that for my house. It was made from white cotton with bright, fresh colours in the print and she'd backed it with a contrasting fabric. Even the binding echoed the blues in the quilt.

Then I noticed one of Delphine's designs — a fairy quilt. I remembered her telling me that she hoped to extend her tea dress range to include fairytale designs for quilts and dolls.

In that moment, Ewan's voice resonated towards me in the shop. The customer had gone. We were alone.

'Beautiful quilt, isn't it?' he said.

I looked over at him. He stood beside the counter, leaning casually, looking so cool and handsome in his white shirt and cinnamon–coloured trousers. The intense blue of his eyes made me wonder if he wore contacts. Who had eyes as blue as that?

He grinned at me. 'Are you okay? You seemed rather...distracted.'

He'd got that right.

The roguish dimples in his cheeks deepened.

Speak. Say something, I urged myself. But I could only gaze at him and wonder why his ex–girlfriend had been foolish enough to ever leave him. Though if I was being honest, really honest, I was glad she had. Ewan was now single. I didn't think that I could replace her. Not me. But a girl can dream.

'Is there something in particular you were looking for?' he said, jolting me from my wayward thoughts. 'Do you see anything in the shop that takes your fancy?'

Yes, you.

'I, eh...I came to pick up my order. I placed an order online for a duvet cover, a patchwork quilt and —'

'A doll,' he finished for me. 'I have them here.' He pulled them from a shelf behind the counter. 'Would you like the name tag for the doll or would the child prefer to name the doll?'

Child? What child? Oh, right. 'Erm, no. The doll is for me. I don't have a child. I'm not married or involved or...' Shut up, I scolded myself. 'It's to match my living room decor.'

'The dolls are very popular as decor accessories,' he said, though I'm sure I caught a smirk in those dimpled cheeks.

He held the doll up and adjusted her hair that was woven from light blue wool. Her face had soft features and rosy cheeks. She was made from various cotton print fabrics and her dress had tiny fairies, butterflies and flowers on it.

'She's lovely,' he said, popping her into a bag while looking straight at me.

Did I just get a compliment from him? He was meaning the doll, wasn't he?

The sexy smile was still there as he dropped her name tag into the bag. 'You'll probably name her, but I'll give you her name tag anyway.'

'What's her name?'

'Veronica Blue. Named after a flower apparently. She's part of a new range of rag dolls and fairy dolls.'

'Veronica it is then,' I said, deciding it suited her perfectly.

He began to fold the patchwork quilt and then stopped. 'Would you prefer the tea shop quilt? There's no problem if you'd rather have it instead of the patchwork. You seemed quite taken with Agnes' quilt. I assume you've recently started working for her at the knitting shop.'

'Yes and no, not quite.'

He tried not to laugh.

'What I mean is...yes, I'd prefer the tea shop quilt even though the patchwork is nice. And no, I'm not working at the knitting shop. I'm a marketing consultant and helping Agnes with her business.'

I thought he'd ask me about her leasing the new shop, or about me being her marketing consultant, but no. He became quiet. Had I said something wrong?

He put the patchwork quilt aside and came over to where I was standing. My goodness he was gorgeous. And tall, and sexy, and... I needed some air.

I studied him while he picked up the tea shop quilt, folded it carefully and put it in a bag. Then he added the duvet cover I'd bought. He put the two bags side by side on the counter.

I went over to the counter aware of the curious gaze from those amazing blue eyes. I went to lift the bags as he reached over the counter to give them to me and our hands brushed against each other.

I pulled my hands away, as if I'd been scalded, and in a way I had. A frisson had gone through me at his touch. I was keyed up, it was a stifling hot day and he was totally gorgeous. The combination threw me for a loop but I made a huge effort to appear unperturbed by the effect he had on me, smiled politely, picked up the bags and went to leave.

I got as far as the door when he called to me. 'Wait a moment, Tilsie.'

Hearing him say my name sent a wave of excitement through me. But of course my name was on the order.

He hurried from behind the counter, closing the gap between us, towering above me in all his classy handsomeness.

'You could be just the person I've been needing to help me with my business,' he said. His broad shoulders shaded out part of the sunlight that streamed through the doorway. Up close, I could see the smooth texture of his golden tanned skin that was exposed from having the two top buttons of his shirt undone. No complaints from me. I couldn't remember the last time I'd seen such an attractive–looking man. On cold rainy days this would be a warm memory to think back on.

He smiled down at me. 'What do you think, Tilsie? Would you consider helping me? I'd like to create some brochures for the shop.'

'Brochures? You'd be far better off adding features to your website. Customers would be interested in reading those. Your website is efficient but I couldn't help but notice that it's a bit empty. There were no newsy details of items you have in stock or what's going to be coming in for other seasons.'

'See, I do need you. When can you start?'

'I think I just have.'

We smiled at each other.

'I'm busy with the shop, as I'm sure you are with your marketing work, but I'm free this evening after I shut the shop at five if you're available to meet.'

I knew what my schedule was and nodded that I was available. Although I had a pretty packed schedule I was up–to–date with things, and making time to meet up with Ewan seemed more like a pleasure than work.

'Shall we say just after five o'clock?'

'I'll come back then,' I agreed. 'It would help if I could have a look at the range of products you have in stock.'

He frowned and ran a hand through his silky dark hair. 'That's the thing — most of my stock is kept at my house in the niche.'

'The niche?'

'I live in what is lovingly known as the hidden niche. It's only ten minutes drive from the city centre but it feels like living the rural life. Most people have never heard of it and that's fine by me and the others who live there.'

'It sounds idyllic.'

'It is. It's like something you'd see in a picture postcard of a quaint little community of cottages and converted coach houses. I stay in one of the old coach houses. I moved in years ago and can't imagine living in the city centre again. The property has plenty of room to live comfortably and accommodate the stock for the shop. I'm not trying to entice you to come to my house, but it really would be more convenient if you could pop along and see all the stock. I have new items that I haven't even uploaded for sale yet on my website. It's been hectic recently. Customers have been buying up the cool bed linen, especially in this hot weather. I had to order in more from my supplier — and that was what I wanted to talk to Agnes about. I wondered if she could sew two quilted bed runners to match the summer range of the duvet covers for my window display.

I had asked Delphine to supply them but unfortunately she's up to her eyeballs in creating vintage tea dress fashions for summer.'

I explained that I knew Delphine and had done some marketing for her.

'Well then, you'll understand how busy we all are, but we try to help each other. What's good for one business is generally beneficial to another.'

'I'll come along to your house this evening.'

He smiled. 'Great. Do you like cake? The cake shop next door sells an amazing range. I've yet to ask for one they don't have. I could buy us a cake before closing and we can have that in the garden later.'

The offer just got better and better. If he'd asked me to move in for a week's holiday I think I'd have agreed.

'A cake would be lovely, Ewan.'

'What type would you like?'

I shrugged happily. 'Any type. A cream sponge, chocolate cake, lemon...I don't mind. I enjoy baking and I have rarely had a cake I don't like.'

'Baking, huh? Maybe you can suggest a cake that they won't have. It's a silly ongoing thing we do. They've beaten me every time. What do you suggest that could flummox them?'

As I'd been thinking about baking one, I suggested my favourite. 'A confetti cake.'

The blue of his eyes sparked as if I'd ignited a reaction in him. 'Wedding cake?'

'No, it's just the name of a sponge cake that's baked with colourful sprinkles through the mix and makes it look like confetti.'

'That's okay then.' He breathed a sigh of relief. 'I'm allergic to the whole idea of weddings. I'm not the marrying kind.'

I don't know why I felt deeply disappointed. Why should I care? But I did.

'Ask them for any cake you like if the confetti cake bothers you.'

'No, not at all. Perhaps I'll finally beat them. They pride themselves on having a vast range of cakes but I doubt they'll have confetti cake.'

'If they don't have it, I'd be happy to have any cake. Perhaps something with strawberries and summer fruits with fresh cream.'

Having armed Ewan with a back–up suggestion on the cake front, I agreed to meet him later and drove off with my new duvet cover, tea shop quilt and Veronica Blue doll, wondering if there was a reason why he was so against the idea of marriage.

Ewan held up a cake box as I drove up to his shop later that evening. It was a hot, muggy night and the amber glow from the fading sun made the city streets shimmer in a heat haze. I had the car windows open for air.

Ewan leaned down and spoke to me. Another button of his shirt was undone. Deliberate or not, it had the desired effect. I tried to focus on the white cake box he was pointing to rather than his manly chest.

'Confetti cake,' he said.

'Thwarted again. Never mind. It'll be delicious.'

He smiled at me. 'Do you want to come with me in my car?'

'No, I'll follow you in mine.'

'What's your phone number in case you get lost. Once we get to the narrow opening in the trees it's like driving into a forgotten niche. No one ever finds it easily. I drove around for an hour before I ever found the route in.'

'I'll keep up with you.' But I gave him my number anyway.

I followed him as he drove his four–by–four car through the city and took one of the main roads that led to the outskirts. From there we took a route through an area thick with trees and countryside lanes with tall grass and wildflowers lining the edges. I wondered how he ever got home during winter nights when it was snowing, but I guessed his car could handle the terrain, and in an entire year there were only a handful of days when the snow was heavy enough to really affect the traffic. A worthwhile inconvenience to live in this hidden wonderland.

I kept the windows down and occasionally the wildflower fronds brushed against my hand as they reached into the car. The air was filled with the scent of blossoms and grass. Any stresses of the day felt watered down, as if I'd left them behind in the city while venturing into another world. The work and stress would be there for me when I returned to the city, but for now I was happy to breathe easier than I had in months.

The road narrowed further before opening out into a main street. The street was as I'd imagined it would be.

It had a scattering of old–fashioned cottages and houses and a cluster of shops in the main part of the street. We drove past a newsagents and grocers and a tiny bakery to arrive outside Ewan's white–painted coach house. In its heyday I supposed it had been a livery stable and house combined. The conversion had kept the beauty of the architecture while bringing it into the modern world in such a way that it wasn't an intrusion. It blended in with everything even though it was the largest building in the street.

We got out of our cars and I followed Ewan up the flower–filled pathway of his front garden.

This man had roses round the door. Pinch me I was dreaming. But no, this was for real. If only Ewan was the same. Somehow knowing that he wasn't the marrying kind bothered me more than it should have, and made him seem slightly out of situ in this environment. I pictured that a man in his position would be the type to marry and have a family with children playing in this wonderful garden and the house filled with laughter.

'I'll get the kettle on,' he said, 'and we'll make short work of this cake.'

'I'm glad to see you have your priorities right,' I teased him.

'Too right. Tea, cake, business.'

Inside his house was cool, subdued and manly by design. Dark neutral tones dominated the hallway and staircase. I caught a glimpse of the front lounge as we headed along the hall into the kitchen. The lounge was shaded with velvet drapes. Very classy.

The kitchen was aglow with mellow sunlight and this part of the house, the back of it, was more to my liking — brighter, airy, less formal. Although he had a modern fitted kitchen the traditional touches such as vintage tea towels, an enamel biscuit barrel, ceramic milk jugs, copper pans and baking bowls gave it the modern vintage vibe of his shop.

'Do you bake?' I asked him.

'I think about it, but then I buy cakes from a shop. I never have time for anything other than work these days.'

He filled the kettle and I watched him work at the sink with the light coming in the window, emphasising his strong silhouette. He was almost too tall for his own kitchen. The garden beyond looked trimmed as far as it would allow anyone to tame it. Contained but still wild. How I always wanted to be but never was.

'And in past days?'

'I used to spend most of my life outdoors — climbing, mountaineering, sports. Time out on the hill walks seemed to stretch for hours on end. An afternoon felt like a proper afternoon when time moved at the right pace. Now, blink and it's 3:00 p.m. Where does the time go? There's never enough of it these days.' He glanced at the clock on the kitchen wall which indicated that it was 2:30 p.m.

'It stopped one day at Christmas and I've never wanted to correct it. When I'm home I try not to think about the time. 2:30.p.m is an ideal time.'

The kettle started to boil.

'Can I help?' I offered.

'You could do the honour of cutting the cake.' He pulled out a cake knife from the dresser drawer and handed it to me. 'Plates are in the cupboard.'

I set the cake on a plate and cut a large slice. I lifted the slice carefully on to a side plate.

'Oh great. I hate it when people cut those thin wedges. I prefer a man–size chunk.'

I blinked at him. 'This is my slice.'

Was I joking? He wasn't sure. And then he laughed when he saw me trying not to smile.

We sat outside at a table in the garden enjoying the remnants of the summer evening.

'What do you think of the confetti cake?' I asked him.

'Mmm, this is delicious. I can see why this would be a favourite of yours.'

We enjoyed our tea and cake and chatted about his business.

'I'll show you the stock later. I've already got the new ranges for autumn and some items for winter, especially the Christmas range.'

'On evenings like this, Christmas seems so far off, but I know how quickly the time goes in. I do love Christmas though.'

'Me too. I'm hoping the larger shop will let me expand the new range of bed linen and items such as the table covers and runners for Christmas. My main problem of course is where to take the business from here. Online sales I suppose could be increased. I'd like to have other shops but then I'd have to employ managers to run them. I have one man, a semi–retired businessman who is also a friend of the family, and he looks after my shop when I have to go away on business trips. I'm never away for longer than two or three weeks and he's very reliable and trustworthy. He spent years in the shop trade and knows everything about retail, but I'd prefer to run my own shop and expand other aspects of my business.'

'Such as the online sales?'

'Yes. That way I wouldn't need other shops and I'd be free to increase my stock with specialist items from my suppliers. They're mainly crafters, each specialising in a range of products from bed linen to cushion covers and lamps to one–off rag dolls and hobby horses. These are always popular at Christmas.'

We finished our tea and cake, and chatted some more about the finer points of his marketing, but all the while I wished that time would stand still and that I could enjoy sitting in his garden on this wonderful warm evening. The air was without a breeze, causing the scent from the flowers, and maple, cherry and pear trees to mingle potently with the fading sunlight. He also had a raspberry patch lush with ripe fruit that he didn't have the time or inclination to savour. Those raspberries, had they been in my garden, wouldn't have lasted. I'd have eaten them for breakfast and dinner.

He caught me looking at them.

'Help yourself to the raspberries before you leave,' he said. 'They grow quicker than I can eat them.'

'Thanks, I'll do that.'

He got up and carried our empty teacups and tea tray into the kitchen. I followed him.

He put them down on the kitchen table and continued to lead the way through the hallway to another part of the house.

'The stockrooms are through here,' he said.

What once may have been a drawing room was stacked with boxes and the shelves were full of quilts, table covers, bed linen and other items ready to be sold in his shop or online. It was very organised and yet packed so tightly that I had to stand close to him in the centre of the room where he had a computer set up to log all the stock.

He tapped in a few numbers and then scrolled down the items to let me see how many things he had available. I bent beneath his arm to peer at the screen.

'The Christmas selection is fantastic,' I said.

'I think I've got a number of ranges that will be popular. Some years the trends are stronger than others. This year feels like a winner.'

I took in everything I could, mentally calculating how to grasp hold of all of this and present it on his website so that customers could feel as I did — that I wanted to buy almost everything I saw.

'I can't make up my mind what range I like the most,' I told him.

'I've got several new suppliers and the deals I have with them suits all our interests while keeping the items affordable for customers. Obviously with the high quality of the fabrics, designs and workmanship, they cost a little more, but customers expect to pay a bit extra for this type of quality.'

As we turned away from the computer we brushed against each other, and laughed as we both clumsily couldn't get out of each other's way without contact.

'There's not much room in here,' he apologised. 'The other stockroom is through the back. It's smaller and packed to the gunnels with orders. I have a couple of people from down the road who come in and pack up the online orders and post them off by courier to customers, but it's become hectic this summer. I'll probably have to hire extra hands to help when the Christmas orders come pouring in.'

I nodded thoughtfully. 'Where do you eventually see your business? You surely can't keep up with this type of demand indefinitely without expanding your distribution methods.'

'You're right, but for the past ten months I've been casting my net wider and have almost secured some bigger clients — a couple of hotel and restaurant chains. Boutique types, mid–range but upmarket enough to want the type of look for their hotels and restaurants that my stock can give them. The specialist items interest them. Sometimes a cocktail bar and restaurant needs just the right look for its clients. Honeymoon suites at some of the hotels are always on the lookout for the latest trends to refresh their styling.'

I smiled. The man who was allergic to even the mention of marriage was kitting out honeymoon suites.

'Go on, say it, Tilsie.'

'I'm not saying a word.'

'Just because I'm not a marriage type of man, it doesn't mean that I can't supply honeymooners with luxurious, handmade satin quilts that will make their wedding nights that little bit more special.'

Several quilts that looked like they would make any couple's night more sensual were within touching distance from me. I trailed the tips of my fingers along the satin–stitched seams letting my imagination wonder if nights like that lay ahead for me.

Chapter Four

Vintage Designs

It was almost midnight by the time I finished trawling through all the stock that Ewan had and discussing ideas for his marketing. I'd worked with a couple of businesses like his before so I already had a rough plan of what would work for him.

'I should've cooked dinner for us,' he said as I was leaving.

We'd had another couple of rounds of tea and scoffed the confetti cake between us. I was well fuelled up on tea and cake.

'The tea and cake was fine, Ewan.' I stepped out into the front garden with a butter tub full of the raspberries he'd given me. The scent from the roses was heady and the street was so quiet I felt the need to keep my voice down not to disturb anyone.

Ewan followed me out, having grabbed his car keys. He insisted on leading me out of the hidden niche as far as the main road into the city centre so that I didn't get lost.

I got into my car, started up the engine and rolled the window down. The night air was so still and hot.

Ewan leaned down and spoke to me. 'Thanks again for all the suggestions for the marketing. I feel inspired. I can't wait to get started on updating my website. How long do you think it'll take for you to write the copy for the main descriptions?'

'A few days. I'll email it to you.' We'd agreed that he had too many items for each product to be given a full description, so I suggested he divide the items into categories such as quilts, cushions, home accessories and give each of these a detailed description that would explain about the quality of the work, the fabric and the design. I'd written copy for clients during my corporate marketing work and offered to write these for him.

He smiled, tapped the top of the car and walked away. 'We'll drive back the way we came in.' He got into his car and I followed him along the grassy roadway that eventually opened out into the main thoroughfare. He drove as far as the first roundabout. I drove off and headed into the city while he continued back round and disappeared into the niche again.

As I drove through the city streets my mind was full of thoughts about what I'd write for him, and even when I arrived home, got ready for bed and turned off the bedside lamp, I found it difficult to stop thinking about Ewan. I loved his house and his garden. Apart from the roses it had some of my favourite flowers — mignonette. Such pretty little flowers with a potent fragrance, especially in the evening. I had them in my garden which was tiny in comparison to his. I didn't have any time to tend to the flowers I used to love. Life had become so hectic I'd even hired someone to cut my lawn for me.

And as I lay there in bed I wondered...had I made the right decision to give up my past career and go it alone? Back then, I had most evenings and weekends off. Now that I worked for myself everything merged into one continuous workload that never really ended. Certainly, I'd made time for my knitting, but there was time for little else. Perhaps I needed to reassess my own marketing plan so that there was time to enjoy myself as well as work hard. No easy task.

I realised I'd have to wait a while before I could ease back on the workload. Maybe by late autumn? Another summer gone, filled with work and...what else? No romance. No one special to share it with. No one had replaced my ex. Had I made the right decision? Had I? The past two years had slipped by so quickly that I could remember every last word we'd thrown at each other during our final meeting to split up.

'You're a fool, Tilsie,' he'd snapped at me. 'You're one of the best marketers the company has. You've got an executive position and you're throwing it away to become self–employed.' He shook his head and picked up the last of his bags.

'I'm not happy,' I told him.

'What's happy got to do with it? Happy doesn't pay the bills. Happy doesn't bring you financial security or time off.' He shook his head again, threw his keys on the table and muttered as he walked away. 'I'll give it a year, no, two years because you're stubborn. Two years from now you'll be lying in bed at night wondering why the hell you threw everything you had away.'

Damn him, damn him.

Blink and my alarm went off. I woke up exhausted from the heat, disturbed by uneasy dreams, and with the feeling that I'd barely closed my eyes and it was time to get up and start another busy day.

The new duvet cover, quilt and doll lay unpacked where I'd left them. I hadn't even checked to see what Agnes had dropped into my bag of wool. Where was the bag of wool? I wasn't sure where I'd left it.

I checked my schedule on the laptop. I had a meeting with a client in less than an hour.

I jumped in the shower, skipped breakfast, except for a handful of the raspberries, grabbed the paperwork for the meeting and drove off in time to secure the deal and advise them on their advertising promotion.

I stopped for an early lunch in the car — a takeaway tea and salad sandwiches with crisp lettuce and cherry tomatoes. I parked under a tree to shade out the blazing sunlight and was glad that I'd worn a lightweight white cotton shirt and blue skirt.

It was while sitting there that I realised I'd left the bag of wool on the back seat of the car. I reached over and had a look inside. The wool to make the snowman and the wrap glittered in the daylight. Oh how I wished I had the time to sit and knit something as cute at the snowman with his smiling face and little hat and scarf. But I would. Once the day's work was done, I'd start knitting him. The wrap would take more time. The snowman was achievable in a day. Then I saw something else glittering beneath the aquamarine yarn for the cowl. I pulled out a small bag that contained a kit to make a knitting bee brooch. I smiled when I saw it. Agnes was so kind and welcoming. The knitting bee ladies made brooches of various styles and colours from felt and yarn. The brooches weren't worn as badges, just pretty accessories that were fun to make and could be worn at any time.

The kit Agnes had chosen blended with the wool I'd bought — white and silver with gold metallic yarn. Diamante gems sparkled in the sunlight and a leaflet gave instructions on how to make the brooch. It was made from a template design that I had to embroider with the yarn and decorate with diamante and crystal beads. I would make the brooch later, I told myself. And make a start on the snowman.

My ex didn't have to be right. I could make my life whatever I wanted it to be. I didn't regret giving up my corporate career and I certainly didn't miss him. There would be someone else out there for me. There would. There definitely would.

My phone rang.

'Hello, is that Tilsie?' a man said.

'Yes, who is this?' At first I thought it was Ewan and then I realised it wasn't. But there was something vaguely familiar about this voice. Sexy, sophisticated and yet cold–edged.

'It's Stewarton. Can we meet? I'd like to talk to you about something.'

Stewarton? What the...?

'I got your number from your website. Are you available this afternoon?'

'Eh, no. I'm busy all day.'

'This evening?'

'Well I'd planned to...' *to what? Make a snowman and a knitting bee brooch.*

'Dinner. Have dinner with me. I understand that you're busy but you'll have to eat. We can chat over dinner.'

'Chat about what?'

'About Julie's plan to approach Mr Feingold and override Agnes' agreement for the vacant shop.'

'Have you spoken to Agnes?'

'No. You said that you were handling things for her, so I assumed you'd be the one I'd deal with.'

'Deal with? You make it sound as if we'll have some sort of argument over the lease.'

'No, what I have to tell you is in both our interests. Shall we say seven–thirty at the new restaurant along from Ewan's shop?'

I knew the restaurant. Very upmarket. I hadn't been in but I'd heard the food was wonderful.

'Can we make it eight. I have a client's meeting at six and it could run late.' And I wanted time to pop home to change before having a dinner assignation with Stewarton.

'See you at eight, Tilsie.'

I clicked the phone off and put the knitting bee brooch kit back into the bag of wool. I sighed and tucked the bag behind the seat. The knitting would have to wait.

I made a quick detour to Agnes' shop to tell her about my meeting with Stewarton and to warn her that Julie had plans to thwart her business and had no intention of going quietly into the night.

'Julie can go and take a run and jump to herself,' said Agnes. 'She can't have the shop. Mr Feingold has promised it to me.'

'I don't know what Julie has in mind but I'm having dinner with Stewarton tonight to discuss it. I thought I should let you know.'

Agnes' eyes twinkled behind her spectacles. 'Dinner with Stewarton?'

'It's not like that. He wanted to talk to me about Julie and as we're both so busy we decided to chat over dinner.'

'Where is he taking you?'

'To the new restaurant along from Ewan's shop. He sounded as if he knew Ewan but I suppose he's sussed out all the businesses around here on Julie's behalf. What type of businesses does Stewarton have?'

'Financial advisor type businesses. A couple of posh offices where only those with lots of money to spend dare step inside. He doesn't have a shop like mine where there is stock. Nothing like that. He advises his clients about their finances. By all accounts he's rich from various investments he made when he was younger. He seems to have a knack for numbers.'

'He's in the right business by the sounds of it.'

'Yes, and he's capable of using his money and power to help that girlfriend of his dabble in her silly whims. It's the trouble she'll cause. She'll just walk away when she realises that a shop like this, a knitting shop with all these haberdashery items, takes a ton of work and dedication. She'll get someone else to handle it and then lose interest and offload the whole thing to Stewarton to tidy up the mess.'

'I'll try to talk some sense into Stewarton. If he's got an analytical financial mind maybe he'll see logic and advise Julie to do something else.'

Agnes gave my hand a gentle grasp. 'Do your best, Tilsie. I'll be here working late so you can drop by after dinner and tell me all about it. I've had a load of new yarn in and vintage patterns that need sorting out.' She pointed to a large cardboard box brimming with paper patterns.

'Are those vintage dress patterns as well as knitting patterns?' I was sure I could see tea dress patterns and stylish skirt suits from the 1940s and 1950s peeking out from the woolly jumper, bobble hat and tea cosy patterns.

Agnes gently pulled two of the dress patterns from the box. 'Yes, they were in with the knitting patterns so I thought I'd make them available too. Some of them are a bit tattered around the edges or too fragile for sale, but I'll mend them and make use of them. Let me know if you want any. I have lots of patterns.'

'Thanks. I was thinking that when my work is settled I'd like to sew as well as knit.' I peered at the various items. 'I quite like the look of that vintage jumper pattern. You don't see patterns like that nowadays.'

'I'll put the jumper pattern aside for you, and there's a bobble hat to match it.'

I checked the time. 'I have to run. I've another client to meet.'

'Let me know what happens with Stewarton. Doesn't matter how late it is. I'll be here until midnight and the kettle is always on for a cup of tea.' She waved me off with a parting piece of advice. 'Don't let the eye candy fool you. Stewarton's a cool customer and knows how to use his looks to woo the ladies.' She gave me a knowing wink.

The afternoon went well. My clients were happy with their marketing campaigns, but the time flew in and before I knew it I was sitting at the last meeting of the day at six o'clock. Thankfully, the meeting didn't drag on so I was able to drive home, shower and get ready for my dinner date with Stewarton. Though it wasn't a date, I corrected myself. Even though Stewarton was handsome with a voice as smooth as single malt, I wouldn't let the eye candy detract from the point of the meeting — to defend Agnes' business from Julie's underhanded plans.

The restaurant felt cool with an airy but expensive decor with plenty of greenery. Although I'd geared myself up to tackle Stewarton, I was looking forward to sitting down to a sophisticated dinner and relaxing after a hectic day.

Stewarton was dressed in a well–cut grey suit and white shirt and tie. He welcomed me when I walked in. At least I think he did. He didn't smile. That handsome face of his didn't give anything away. I'd always been quite adept at reading people, but Stewarton's reserve gave me nothing to go on.

We sat at a table for two and selected from the menu while our drinks were served. We both opted for an iced fruit cocktail that had a smidgen of alcohol to allow us to drive home after dinner rather than share a taxi.

I chose a delicate pasta dish with roast vegetables and a savoury sauce that was one of the evening's specialities. Stewarton had seared fish that looked as appetising as he confirmed it tasted.

The formalities over, we began to chat while enjoying our meal. I let him open the conversation. Thankfully he got straight to the point which I preferred.

'Julie is determined to approach Mr Feingold and offer to pay double the amount for the lease.'

I cut into my food. 'As I explained to you, the agreement is already finalised. The shop lease belongs to Agnes and no amount of haggling is going to alter that fact. Mr Feingold isn't the type, by reputation, to renege on the deal.'

Stewarton nodded and concentrated on his meal.

'If you agree with me then why are we here discussing something we both know is futile?'

The stunning grey eyes looked over at me, causing a reaction in the pit on my stomach that I hadn't expected. He was handsome, no doubt about it, but for the first time I thought I saw a flicker of him, the man behind the suit. I didn't think that he was a facade. In fact, I sensed the opposite. Stewarton was exactly what he appeared to be — a powerful financial businessman. But somewhere deep inside him there was the man who loved Julie, and I thought I caught a glimpse of that side of his nature for the briefest moment.

'I promised Julie that I would try to help her. I like to think that I'm a man of my word, so this is me keeping my promise to her that I would try to find a way to help secure her shop premises.' The broad shoulders shrugged beneath his jacket. I'd worn a sleeveless, vintage lemon linen dress that was both cool and sophisticated enough for a restaurant like this, but he looked cooler than me even with his jacket on.

'At least you're loyal.' I probably sounded surprised.

His eyes searched deep into mine. 'What would make you think I wouldn't be?'

'Oh, I don't know...' The cut–throat businessman in him. The financial mind that could tot up the unfair odds against Agnes winning against a powerful man like him. And Julie. He loved Julie. Although I'd never met her, everything I'd heard made me picture a vixen, as Agnes had described, who was quite happy to ruin another woman's hard–earned knitting shop on a whim. But he loved this harridan and that said a lot about him.

'Julie wants to own a shop and I really am going to try to help her.'

'If you really want to help her you should encourage her to rethink owning a knitting shop. Julie doesn't knit. She doesn't know anything about knitting patterns or sewing. How could she advise customers? She'd have to rely on hiring someone with experience to deal with them. It's a ridiculous pipedream. The whole idea seems like a whim that won't even last until Christmas, then you'll have to sort out all the mess and get rid of the shop for her. You'd be far better getting something less permanent. A pop–up shop in one of the large department stores would be better. Then when Julie is fed up and realises that it takes a lot of hard work to run a shop, even a pop–up, her venture could be folded easily without ruining anyone else's business.'

'A pop–up shop.' He sounded interested. 'That's a great idea.'

'And if Julie is the type I think she is, then she'd be better suited to having a fashion outlet rather than knitting or anything vintage. High fashion would work for her. That's what I'd advise her to do, though you know her well and I don't.'

'No, you're right. A pop–up fashion shop right in the centre of the city. That would be ideal. Julie would love that. I'm sure she would. It wouldn't last. We all know that. However, as it's a pop–up it could be dealt with so much easier. I wish I'd thought of that.'

We ate our meal in silence for a couple of minutes and I imagined his mind ticking over the pop–up options. Then he said, 'Do you enjoy working as a freelance marketer, or do you see yourself venturing into corporate life?'

'I've been there.' I explained about my past experience and somehow that brought up about my ex.

39

'If you weren't happy in the corporate world he should have tried to support your decision even if he thought you'd only try it for two years. I know I would have.'

And all of a sudden the atmosphere changed, as if he'd said something out of turn, a private thought that shouldn't have been uttered.

He appeared flustered for the first time and I think he was grateful that the waiter cleared away our plates and we were given a choice of delicious puddings.

I opted for a fancy ice cream confection. I didn't think Stewarton would have the same but he did. I half wondered if he knew what he'd let himself in for. According to the menu this had numerous layers of ice cream, whipped cream, fresh fruit, sprinkles and all sorts of deliciousness.

The waiter nodded politely and hurried off, leaving us still with that sense of uneasiness between us.

'We don't have to be enemies, Tilsie.'

'I wasn't aware that we were.'

He smiled. I wasn't sure if smiling suited him. The dark brooding look he had was definitely sexier.

'It's probably totally inappropriate to mention under the present circumstances,' he began, 'but I'm organising my company's annual conference. As a marketing consultant, perhaps you'd be interested in coming along? It's not until the last week in November but it doubles as our Christmas event.'

My first reaction was that it would be out of my league. High–powered financial types discussing deals that cost more than the mortgage on my house. 'I don't think so.'

'There's a substantial fee,' he said.

'I couldn't afford it. I'll give it a miss.'

'No, you don't understand. There's a fee paid to guest speakers — experts in finance, marketing, international trade, business advisors.'

I hesitated. Had he just invited me to be one of the guest speakers?

He read my expression. 'Yes, that's right. I'd like you to come along during the weekend event and give a talk on the Friday, Saturday and Sunday on corporate marketing versus independent marketing. I think it would be of great interest to many of my clients and others at the conference. I try to have different speakers every year. What do you say?'

I didn't know. I had given presentations during my corporate work and getting up in front of people to talk about marketing didn't bother me. I liked my marketing.

While I swithered, Stewarton jotted down his private number on the back of his business card. Call me nearer the time, or I'll call you around the beginning of November. He also scribbled a ballpark figure of the amount I'd be paid to give three talks during the weekend conference at a large mansion on a private estate that was hired out for events like this.

He pushed the card across the table and I gulped when I saw the amount. 'You're kidding me.'

He shook his head. 'Nope. Speakers are well paid. I pay for the best. Guests expect their money's worth at my conferences and that's what I give them.'

'But I'm...'

'Damn intelligent and have extensive knowledge of both ends of the marketing spectrum. Corporate and craft. Experience and knowledge.' He pushed the card further until it touched my fingertips. 'Keep it. Think it over. It's a long time until November, Tilsie. A lot can change by then.'

I put the card in my purse. 'No promises.'

'None taken.'

Our ice cream confections were served. I sat back in my chair as a crystal–cut tall glass filled with layers of ice cream, fruit and every delicious temptation I could dream of was placed in front of me along with the longest silver spoon I'd ever seen. I didn't know whether to laugh or not. Somehow I managed to keep a straight face until the waiting staff had gone so as not to offend them. It wasn't so much the ice cream that made me want to burst out laughing as Stewarton's face when he saw what he was supposed to tuck into.

But then he totally surprised me by picking up his spoon and saying, 'Where do I start?'

'The cherry on the top,' I suggested. My spoon was poised above mine.

'I'm not particularly a cherry type of man but I do love strawberries.'

41

Several strawberries decorated the edges and were sprinkled with crystallized sugar frosting.

'I'll exchange my cherry for one of your strawberries,' he said.

I smiled at him. 'Deal.'

We did a wobbly exchange where I almost dropped the strawberry I'd fished out of the whipped cream.

Stewarton had a steadier hand and put the cherry smack on top of my ice cream.

I couldn't stop smiling.

'What's so amusing?' he said, smiling back at me.

'You. You and your posh executive suit eating the most extravagant ice cream mountain I've ever seen. I'm sorry, Stewarton, but you just don't seem the type.'

'What type do you think I am?'

'More crème brûlée or champagne truffles.'

'That's a compliment, isn't it?'

I laughed. 'It depends.'

'Depends on what?'

'On whether you're a snobby suit with a hoity–toity attitude or whether you're really down to earth and okay with eating frivolous things.'

'Oh I'm definitely a snobby suit. No doubt about it. Not sure about the hoity–toity attitude. Hopefully not.'

I laughed again at him and then tucked into my pudding.

'I was brought up snobby,' he continued. 'That's my excuse. My parents are very well–off. I had a private education and there was never any question that I'd be anything other than rich, successful and working in finance. It worked for my parents. My father was a financier and my parents had a happy marriage. A happy marriage and family life is something I hope to achieve.'

'So you're the marrying kind?' The words were out before I realised what I'd said.

He looked right at me. 'Unlike Ewan.'

My spoon clattered on the edge of the glass dish.

'Yes, I know Ewan. Our paths have crossed, as they say, a few times over the past few years. We even dated the same girl.'

'Really?'

He toyed with his ice cream. 'Well, I was hoping to date her and we'd had dinner once. Then Ewan asked her out and she chose him rather than me.'

'So you're rivals in romance?'

'I prefer to think of it as a fortunate loss. She ended up cheating on him with his cousin, then decided to get back together with him, but he didn't want her back. She even tried to involve me to make him jealous, but by that time I was already involved with Julie.'

'It's a big small world.'

'It is indeed.'

We were quiet for a moment and then I dared to ask, 'Why do you love Julie?'

'Why does anyone love anyone?'

'I hear she's very attractive.'

'She is. She's quite beautiful. On the outside.'

'And on the inside?'

'A seething pit of insecurities and vindictiveness.'

'But you still love her.'

'I do, though I used to love her more. But I believe in loyalty until the bitter end, and that's sadly where we're headed. We don't have the future together that I'd hope for. Our relationship will end, and with Julie it's bound to be acrimonious.'

'What will you do?'

He threw the question right back at me. 'What did you do when you split with your ex?'

'I got on with my life and my work.'

He dug his spoon deep into the depths of the ice cream and fruit. 'That's what most people do. I'll try to forget the past and get on with things. And hopefully meet someone else who is more like me.'

'Snobby and who likes strawberries?' I said flippantly.

He smiled and then added, 'And who wants to get married and have a family.'

'Does Julie?'

'Goodness no. She says it would ruin her figure.'

I watched him chase a red grape around with his spoon.

'Do you know why Ewan is so against marriage?'

'No. The gossip was that his ex girlfriend cheated on him because he wouldn't ask her to marry him. She thought if he realised how easily she could leave him and find someone else he'd pop the question.'

'That idea backfired.'

'It did. Instead of coming back to an engagement ring she came back to a cold shoulder. Ewan is more ruthless than me, though I've definitely got him beat on the snobbery scale. I couldn't imagine having a shop like his. I'd be quite prepared to sell upmarket items but I think I'd draw the line at fluffy cushions and rag dolls. They're just not for me.'

'I bought one of the dolls and she's lovely.'

'Have I insulted you?'

'A few times.'

'I apologise, Tilsie, but why are you still here?'

'For the ice cream.'

'Not the company?'

'Definitely not the company.'

We both laughed and continued to eat our meal unaware that trouble was heading our way on the highest pair of heels I'd seen in years.

Chapter Five

Delphine & Hetty

Julie came strutting into the restaurant on skyscraper heels and a dress that emphasised every inch of her slender body. It had to be her. I hated to admit that there was a similarity between us, only her clothes were more expensive and her shiny blonde hair was the closest to perfection I'd seen in a long time. She targeted our table. This was not going to end well I thought.

She spoke to Stewarton as if I wasn't even there. 'I was driving past, having had another look at the empty premises next to the knitting shop and I saw your car parked outside this restaurant.' Every level of accusation was audible in her tone.

Piercing blue eyes glared down at me and then she turned the vitriol back to Stewarton. 'Who the hell is this?' she demanded.

'Tilsie and I are discussing business.' He sounded calm but I sensed an undertone of shockwaves.

Julie glared down at me again. 'Get lost.' Her tone was poisonous.

I sat still. 'You're wasting your time,' I told her.

Frown lines crossed her smooth brow. 'What?'

'I've dealt with worse harridans than you, Julie,' I said. 'So you can take your attitude and demands and stick them up your scrawny backside.'

She blinked several times and then said to Stewarton, 'Are you going to let her talk to me like that?'

'Don't cause a scene,' he told her, keeping his voice level. 'Wait for me in the car or drive home and I'll talk to you later.'

'I was at the chateau tonight but that man, Mr Feingold, wouldn't let me have the shop lease,' she said.

'I told you not to do that. I said I'd handle things for you.'

'You were dragging your heels, Stewarton. That silly woman Agnes had already secured the lease. You were too late in sorting things out.' She sighed and glared at him petulantly. 'I wanted that shop. I *wanted* it.'

'I have something in mind that I think you'll prefer.'

She stared at him. 'You're just saying that so I'll leave.'

He shook his head. 'No. I've spoken to a marketing consultant and they suggested something that I know you'll want.'

He'd triggered her curiosity. 'Is it another shop?'

'It's another shop idea, more fashion–based and in a better location.'

She perked up. 'Well then, I'll see you later.' With a final stab of blue daggers at me, she turned and strutted out of the restaurant.

'Marketing consultant, huh?'

He nodded. 'Yes. I should probably pay her for her excellent advice.'

'Consider dinner as payment in full.'

He got up to leave and settle the bill.

Despite everything that had happened, including an encounter with the delightful Julie, I had enjoyed having dinner with Stewarton. I watched him from across the room, and assumed I wouldn't see him again for a long time, perhaps never. There would be no reason for us to meet, not now that Julie wasn't going to move in on Agnes' territory.

Outside the restaurant we said our goodbyes, as if we'd known each other longer.

'Thanks again, Tilsie, for your pop–up shop suggestion and for being reasonable.'

A mild breeze blew along the street and I sensed a chill, a change in circumstances in the air.

'I hope everything works out for you,' I said to him.

'And for you.'

With those words we went our separate ways.

I drove the short distance to Agnes' shop. The lights were on inside and she was busy sorting the window display.

'You told Julie to stick her attitude?' Agnes said when I explained what had happened in the restaurant. 'Oh I'd love to have seen her face. I bet she wasn't used to anyone telling her straight.'

We sat in the knitting shop having tea.

'At least things are settled. Julie is out of the picture.'

Agnes gave me a look. 'What about Stewarton?'

'What about him?' I knew what she was hinting at. Was I interested in him? Did I think that he was handsome and wished that somehow things in life could work out differently and that I'd be the one to date him rather than Julie?

'Is he continuing to date her or do I sense that things were a little bit more than just business tonight between the two of you?'

'He was good company and I saw another side to him that was quite attractive and less strident than I'd imagined.'

'You fancy him then?'

I laughed. 'Are you always so subtle?'

'I can tell by the way you talk about him. He is a handsome creature. It's a shame he's spoken for.'

'He doesn't hold out much hope for his relationship with Julie.' I gave her the details.

'The marrying kind, eh? That's more than Ewan could offer you.'

'Agnes, don't be silly. I'm not getting involved with either of them.'

'Why not?'

'Well, because...' Neither of them had asked me out. I was too busy. I didn't have time to knit a snowman let alone get involved in a relationship.

'Ewan could change his mind about marriage, and besides, not every romance has to last forever even though we'd love them to. You could enjoy a summer romance with Ewan. I know I would given the chance.'

I shook my head. 'My life is busy enough without getting involved with Ewan and ending up with a broken heart again.'

'Love can be complicated at times,' she admitted. 'That's why I take comfort in my knitting and so do a lot of the women who are part of the knitting bee. Knitting eases the stresses and strains of daily life.' She poured us more tea from a teapot covered with a knitted bumblebee tea cosy. The cute little bumble was something else I longed to knit.

'What about you?' I asked her. 'Was there ever a great love of your life? Apart from knitting.'

She smiled at me. 'Once, a long time ago. It seemed like another life back then. He wanted us to get married but I turned him down. It was a mistake. Biggest mistake I ever made.' She shrugged and adjusted the knitted bumblebee on the tea cosy as she cast her thoughts back to the past.

'What happened to him?'

'He married someone else and that was that.'

'Do you still think about him?'

'Not really. I try not to dwell on the past. I never married, never found the man for me, but I've had a few light–hearted romances.'

A car drove up and a woman got out. She opened the boot of her car and lifted out a vintage, cream–coloured wire mannequin and carried it towards the shop.

I recognised them both immediately.

Agnes jumped up and waved excitedly at her. 'Here's Delphine. She's letting me borrow Hetty for the photographs of the yarns and vintage patterns.'

We helped Delphine bring Hetty into the shop. Delphine was around the same age as me and a lovely, grey eyed blonde.

Delphine seemed pleased to see me. 'Long time no see. Agnes says you're helping her with her marketing.'

'Yes. How are things with you?' I said.

'Brilliant. We should find time to chat and catch up with all the news.'

'I'll boil the kettle again for tea,' said Agnes.

'I've got a couple of vintage tea dresses in the car,' said Delphine. She went out and brought them in. One was tea rose pink with a velvet ribbon trim and the other was silver–grey. Both were part of her fairytale collection of dresses from her shop a few streets away.

The silky fabrics glittered under the shop lights. I touched the leaf–shaped cap sleeves on the grey dress. The beadwork dripped like diamonds from the edges, delicate and yet so beautiful, from another era. Each bead was sewn on by hand. Silvery threads entwined themselves through the gossamer grey chiffon of the tea dress that looked at times like a shimmering shadow depending on how the light caught the needlework.

Delphine hung the tea rose dress on a padded satin hanger beside the Christmas display. Santa wobbled but didn't topple over and there wasn't a peep from his squeaker.

'These dresses are gorgeous,' I said.

'Oh they're fantastic,' Agnes agreed. 'I love the wispy fabrics. They'll look great with my knitted cardigans on Hetty.'

Delphine fished out strings of pearls and a sparkly vintage floral brooch from her bag. 'Add these as well. They'll look lovely in the photographs.'

The plan was for Agnes to borrow Hetty for photographs with a vintage theme as part of the launch of the new shop. We'd discussed this, and Delphine had offered to loan her the mannequin.

Agnes poured our tea and I held Hetty steady while Delphine put one of the dresses on the mannequin. The silver–grey one. Then we carried Hetty over to the window display.

Delphine added the jewellery and then stepped back to admire her handiwork.

'What do you think, Agnes?'

'Perfect. I'll give her back within a few days. Thanks for giving me a loan of Hetty.'

'You're welcome. When do you get the keys to the new shop?' Delphine asked.

'Tomorrow. I'm so excited. I can't wait to start adding the stock. Tilsie came up with the vintage theme idea, and I'm going to extend my haberdashery with lots of vintage items including a range of old–fashioned knitting and sewing patterns.'

She showed Delphine the box of patterns.

Delphine immediately picked out one of the 1940s tea dress designs. 'I'll buy this. I have new fabric that would work a treat with this pattern.'

Agnes insisted she take whatever patterns she wanted for free. Delphine chose two, both tea dress designs. One was a wrapover.

We chatted and the conversation included talking about Ewan.

'How is Ewan doing with his new shop?' Delphine asked.

'Fine,' said Agnes. 'Tilsie is helping him with his marketing now too. She's even been to his house for tea and cake.'

Delphine's eyes sparkled with interest. 'I hear he lives in a beautiful old coach house out in the wilds.'

I sipped my tea and told them about Ewan's house. 'It's like something out of a picture postcard. That's what I thought when I saw it. He's even got roses round the front door and I loved his back garden.'

'It's a shame he's not the marrying kind,' said Agnes.

'Few men are,' said Delphine. 'Most of them need a nudge towards commitment.'

49

'I've been trying to encourage Tilsie to have a wild summer fling with Ewan.'

Delphine laughed. 'Are you going to?'

'No, of course not,' I said, wondering why I felt like I was telling a lie.

'Oh I meant to tell you, Tilsie, Mr Feingold phoned earlier this evening,' said Agnes. 'He's sending round a couple of his building men to tear down the partition between my shops tomorrow. He says the stoor will be minimum and they'll put up dust sheets. I thought I'd ask Matt to help me shift the counter and other heavy stuff out of the way. Make use of those muscles of his.'

'That's great, Agnes.'

She nodded excitedly. 'I never thought Mr Feingold would organise things so quickly but the sooner I get the new shop up and running the better.'

I surmised that the visit from Julie might have had something to do with Mr Feingold speeding matters up.

'And he says the men will help with the signage,' Agnes added. 'I couldn't wish for a better landlord.'

'I have to love you and leave you,' said Delphine. 'I've my website to update before I can get to my bed and I don't want to be doing it when I'm tired. I don't want to faff things up like I've done before.'

I promised to drop by Delphine's shop soon for a chat and to see the new dresses she had for sale.

After Delphine left, Agnes knitted a few rows of a baby blanket she was knitting for the shop display while we finished our tea.

'This is a popular item. The pattern is basic. You can knit this wee baby blanket up in a day. I'm using bigger needles but the pattern works just as well with smaller needles to make a tighter–knit blanket.' She nodded at a mini version of the blanket on the counter. 'I include the pattern for a matching doll's blanket to go with it.'

'That's a nice touch.'

As we finished our tea the shop was so quiet late at night that I heard a sound coming from near Santa's knitted grotto. 'What's that noise? It sounds like snoring.'

I got up to take a look and jumped when I saw the fluffy, dark blue wool in the knitting basket display move slightly.

'I forgot to mention,' Agnes said continuing to knit unperturbed, 'I'm kitten sitting for my next door neighbour. Her daughter is getting engaged and there's all the fuss of baking cakes and party arrangements. She's running around sorting everything out for her daughter and asked if I'd take care of Cookie for a few hours.'

I peered into the basket and there was the kitten curled up in the balls of wool. He was a little blue Persian, cute as a button, not much bigger than a 100g ball of wool and just as fluffy. I hadn't even noticed him as his fur blended with the yarn.

I peered closer, tempted to lift him out of his basket and give him a cuddle. 'He's adorable.'

'He is, isn't he? He wouldn't settle earlier in the shop. He tried to claw the beard off of Santa. Then I put him in the basket and he settled fine and went to sleep. He seems to like the comfort of the wool. And it's for display only.'

The kitten snored contentedly unaware of how cute he looked.

Agnes glanced over at him. 'It's surprising the noise that a wee pair of lungs can make. He's hardly the size of a ball of wool yet he snores like a trouper. And you should here him when he wants his dinner. He's got a meow on him like a foghorn.'

I laughed and then tried to keep quiet so as not to disturb him.

'Don't worry,' said Agnes. 'He sleeps through everything. I'm not bringing him in tomorrow when the builders are here, but I've promised to take care of him the day after.'

'Customers will love him.'

'He's a wee sweetie. Thankfully he lives next door to my house so when I have to give him back I'll still get to see him most days.'

I got ready to leave. 'What time do the builders arrive tomorrow?'

'Around ten in the morning. I'm going to put a notice up in the window and close the shop. Customers will understand. It'll only be for a day. A few of the knitting bee girls have volunteered to come round and help me tidy things up and get the new shop in order.'

'I'll pop in to help you, and I'll contact the local newspapers to get the advertising features arranged.'

'Oh, it's so exciting.'

I was getting ready to leave when we saw Matt locking up his shop.

Agnes put her knitting down. 'There's Matt. Wave him to come over.'

I opened the door and waved at Matt. He smiled and headed to the shop.

'Is that a cat in that basket?' he said. 'Are you spinning your own wool from cat's fur now?' He was joking of course. Matt was always joking, but I liked a man with a cheery nature.

Agnes explained about the kitten sitting and then she said, 'I need to ask you a favour, Matt. I need to borrow you and your muscles. I'm having Mr Feingold's builders in tomorrow. Could you come over before ten and help me and the girls move the counter?'

'Sure thing, Agnes. I'll help you out.'

I smiled at him.

He grinned at me. 'What is it?'

'Nothing, Matt.' I didn't like to tell him that despite all the fun that was poked at him, I admired his easy–going nature and readiness to help Agnes without a second thought that he'd have to close his shop while he did so.

'Okay,' he said. 'I'll see the pair of you tomorrow.' And off he went. And so did I.

When I got home I made another tea, realising that I'd become a total tea jenny.

Although it was late, I put the tea shop quilt over the back of my sofa in the living room and propped the Veronica Blue doll up on a chair. I also decided to put the new duvet cover I'd bought from Ewan on my bed before climbing in and flopping down exhausted from the day's events.

I thought about Stewarton and Julie. Had they argued over my dinner with him at the restaurant? Had he sold her on the idea of having a fashionable pop–up shop? I hoped so.

I gazed out at the clear midnight sky. I slept with the bedroom window partially open, glad of the night air wafting in. The new duvet cover felt cool against my skin.

And I thought about Ewan and about Agnes' suggestion that I should enjoy a summer fling with him. Chance would be a fine thing. I doubted Ewan was interested in me. When I really thought about it, I'd picked up more interest from Stewarton during dinner when we'd laughed together. Stewarton had looked at me a couple of times, and under other circumstances, I would've been sure that I'd seen a flicker of romantic interest in his eyes.

I pushed such thoughts from my mind. Get some sleep, I told myself. There was no future for me with Stewarton. As for Ewan...

Get some sleep, I told myself again. I'd almost finished writing the features for Ewan's website and planned to email them off to him in the morning.

I'd checked his website earlier and as far as I could see he hadn't updated any of the product pages. I guessed that he'd been too busy. Or had something else happened to make him change his plans?

Chapter Six

Quilting & Sewing

Light summer rain refreshed the city streets and was gone by lunchtime, replaced with a cloudless blue sky and bright, hot sunlight.

I saw a builders' van parked outside Agnes' shop. I parked my car along from them. A lot of activity was buzzing around inside the premises and they'd already adjusted the frontage sign. They'd moved it nearer the centre of the two shops and put end pieces of white signage to extend it.

Agnes saw me through the shop window and beckoned me in. She unlocked the front door of her original shop.

'Come in,' she said. 'The workmen are nearly finished.'

Two men dressed in overalls were folding up the dust sheets and packing their tools into the van. From what I could see they'd hardly made any mess.

'A sweep and a hoover and the new shop will be ready to rock,' said Agnes.

She'd set up her sewing machine in the far corner and while the builders were busy she'd finished the two quilted bed runners for Ewan's shop. She held one of them up to me. 'What do you think? It's less than perfect but it's for his display. No one will be buying it.'

I tried to see what was less than perfect and couldn't. 'I wish I could quilt like that, Agnes.'

'I've been quilting for years. You learn the knack, and these aqua and lemon colours work so well. Ewan handed in the fabric, so while the shop was shut to customers I ran these up on my sewing machine. I'd made a start on them at home but I thought I'd finish them while the work was going on. I'll drop them off to him later, or I don't suppose you'd hand them into him.'

'Yes, I'll drop them off.' I helped her fold the bed runners and put them into a bag.

'Thanks, Tilsie. It'll let him use them for his shop display while I get on with the hoovering here.'

Lisa and two knitting bee ladies came in to help with the clearing up. I passed them on the way out, intending to go back to help once I'd given the bed runners to Ewan.

His shop door was wide open and he was serving a couple of customers. I went in and waited until they'd gone, trying to resist the urge to buy a set of vintage tea towels that were the prettiest I'd ever seen.

I handed him the bag when the customers had gone. 'Agnes made the bed runners for you.'

He admired her sewing. 'She's made a great job of them.'

I took an end of one of the runners and helped Ewan put it on the duvet he had on display in the window. He hung the other runner over the back of a chair.

'I see she's got the builders in.'

'They've finished taking down the partition and extended her shop sign. All she needs to do now is stock the new shop ready for the photographs.'

'She's having photographs taken?'

'Yes. They're for her website and for advertising in the likes of the paper. Delphine has loaned her Hetty to give a stylish vintage theme.'

'That's the mannequin, isn't it?'

Hetty was infamous. Even Ewan had heard about her.

I nodded. 'The thing about working with so many talented craft folk is that I want to buy too many items. Hetty is wearing a chiffon dress that I'd love to own but I know I'd never really wear it except for a party.' I put the set of tea towels down on the counter. 'And your shop could cost me a fortune if I was in here more often.'

He frowned at the tea towels. 'These aren't actually for sale today.'

'That's fine. It was an impulse buy. I don't need them. I'll put them back where I got them.' I went to lift them up but he grasped hold of them. 'They're on special offer.' His gorgeous aquamarine eyes sparkled with mischief. 'They come with a dinner invitation.'

'Really?' I played along. 'Part of a special promotion?'

He nodded and smiled at me. 'If you're not too busy perhaps you'd like to have dinner with me tonight?'

'A business dinner?' I asked tentatively, hoping it wasn't.

'No, though I will bring up how impressed I am with the features you wrote for me. I'm going to add them to the website later. Apart from that I thought I'd promote something else entirely.'

'What would that be?'

'Me.' He stepped closer and although the breeze blew into the shop my temperature went off the scale. His light blue shirt had two buttons undone to reveal his strong, athletic chest that begged me to run my hands over it. And if dinner went well, perhaps I would.

Hold on, I scolded myself the second such thoughts entered my mind. Was I seriously thinking of going on a date with Ewan? It could only end in heartache.

He towered above me and smiled. 'I've been thinking about you since you came to my house, since you first walked into my shop in fact. Have dinner with me.'

All my resolve melted when he gazed at me. Then I thought — why not? Why shouldn't I enjoy myself with this gorgeous man? I felt myself nod.

'I'll pick you up around eight,' he said. 'There's a favourite restaurant of mine that has a wonderful view of the city at night.'

I gave him my home address and promised I'd be ready.

Giddy with excitement, I went back along to Agnes' shop.

She was busy hoovering, and Lisa and the girls were polishing the counter and dusting the shelves in the new shop.

'You're all flushed, Tilsie,' Agnes commented when I walked in. 'Are you okay?'

'Fine.' My voice was pitched too high to hide my excitement and I told her about my dinner date with Ewan.

'What are you going to wear?' she said. 'You'll have to knock his eyes out.'

'I've got a couple of little black dresses that I always feel comfortable in.'

Lisa and the others overheard our conversation and soon they were all giggling and gossiping about what would happen between Ewan and me. Some of the scenarios had me blushing. 'It's just dinner,' I emphasised. 'I'm not marrying him or jumping into a relationship overnight.'

'With Ewan,' said Lisa, 'I'd forget all the rules and just have fun. That's what luscious men like him are for. I know he's not forever and not the marrying kind, but who cares? Dress up and go out and enjoy yourself, Tilsie. You work hard and you deserve a night of romance and passion.'

'Passion?' a man's voice said. 'That's not the type of word I thought I'd hear in a knitting shop.'

I turned round and there was Stewarton.

Before I could say anything, Agnes blurted out about my date with Ewan. I think she did it on purpose, but meaning well, to make sure I didn't swither when I saw Stewarton.

'I trust you'll have a lovely time,' he said. No smile, no warmth.

'Was there something you wanted?' Agnes asked him.

He looked around the shop. 'I wanted to make sure that the shop alternations had gone ahead. I spoke to Mr Feingold and withdrew any offers that Julie had made to him.' He spoke to her but kept glancing at me as if there was something he wanted to say but couldn't or wouldn't now that he knew about my date with Ewan. Bad timing? I wasn't sure.

'Is Julie happy with the pop–up shop suggestion?' I said, feeling an uneasy atmosphere between us.

'Delighted. She's asked me to arrange a pop–up in one of the fashion stores in the city centre. It'll be advertised in the press soon.'

'I'll probably see her feature in the papers then,' I said.

'Tilsie's arranging for a feature for my new shop in the newspapers,' Agnes told him.

'I'll keep a lookout for it,' he said. 'If Tilsie is handling it, I'm certain it'll be a success. Good luck with the new shop,' he concluded and turned to leave.

At that moment Santa tumbled from the shelf where Agnes had stuffed him out of the way of the building work. He rolled along the floor and stopped near my feet. As I bent down to pick him up his squeaker made a loud and disgusting noise. It sounded as if I'd broken wind when I bent down. I squirmed and blushed.

Stewarton's face bore an expression of horrible surprise.

'It wasn't me, it was Santa,' I told him, pinning the blame on the wonky Father Christmas.

Stewarton glanced at the innocent face of the little Santa and gave me a look of complete disbelief before he left.

If ever an excuse didn't fly.

My bedroom looked like a dust devil had hit it sideways. Clothes were trailed from the wardrobe on their hangers and scattered on the bed. Shoes, handbags and accessories lay where I'd tried them on, having decided they looked hideous, unsuitable, unflattering or all three.

On the plus side, my hair looked okay. I'd pinned it up in a chignon and done my makeup. All that was missing was the right dress and accessories which didn't appear to be anywhere near my wardrobe. Damn it.

On impulse, I phoned Delphine at her Fairytale Tea Dress shop hoping she was still open.

'Tilsie, what's wrong?'

'I have a dinner dress date emergency.' I blurted out the problem.

'Come round and I'll sort you out. I'm working late. When's dinner with Ewan?'

'Eight.'

'Two hours to find you the perfect dress. No problem. I've lots of pretty vintage numbers that you'll love to bits. Hurry round and bring your shoes and bag with you so I can match everything up.'

I grabbed everything I thought I'd need and a few more things besides, threw them in the car, along with myself, and drove to Delphine's shop which wasn't far.

'I've had a look through the rails of dresses in your size,' she said, letting me in before locking the door behind me. 'You're about the same size as me.' She led me over to a rail dripping with gorgeousness. That's the only way to describe these visions of vintage style. Sheer, stylish and oh so beautiful.'

I swooned. 'Thanks, Delphine. I appreciate you doing this. I think it must be the heat, but I've got myself into a flap over this silly date with Ewan.'

'The weather forecast is that tonight is going to be the hottest evening for years. A sizzler.' She smiled at me. 'And having a date with Ewan is a guarantee of this whatever the temperature outside. He's a hottie.'

'I must be crazy to even think about getting involved with him. I'm up to my eyeballs in work and...'

'Relax,' she said calmly, and picked two dresses from the rail — one was a lemon chiffon dreamlike little tea dress that really did look

58

like it belonged in a fairytale. Pale golden threads shimmered through the fabric. I'd thought the silvery–grey dress that Hetty wore was a stunner but this was even more beautiful and definitely going home with me whether I wore it to dinner with Ewan or not. The price made it a steal. I couldn't wait to try it on.

I stepped into the changing room and slipped it on. If ever a dress was made for me this was it. 'I love it,' I called through to her. I stepped out wearing neutral court shoes that were both comfy, classy and worked with any colour of dress.

Delphine smiled and nodded. 'That's definitely a dress for you. How does it feel?' She turned me around to check the fit. 'It hangs perfectly and the length is just right.'

'It feels like a dream. I never thought I'd say that about a dress but it really does.'

'It's a genuine vintage number from the 1930s. You can tell from the styling and there is no overlocking on the seams. Overlocking didn't come in until later on. And there's no washing care label. That's another telltale sign of authenticity.'

She held the second dress up. It was in shades of deep blues that faded to whispery violet. 'Try this on too. I know you love the lemon one, but let's see how this one looks on you. I've a white and silvery one that you have to try too.'

I let her talk me into trying on everything she suggested, not that I was complaining. I started to feel so much better wearing these lovely dresses that had a history of past loves and lives. I pictured that the women who'd worn them had danced at parties, kissed the men they'd loved and enjoyed happy times.

Delphine bought preloved vintage dresses, mended them if needed and turned them into wearable fashions. She also created her own tea dresses and other items from the loveliest selection of fabrics and embellished them with ribbon trims and beading and traditional appliqué. Her shop was well–named. Everything looked like it belonged in a fairytale. She also designed and sold her own collection of paper patterns which had been at the heart of the promotion I'd helped her with the previous year.

Delphine put the lemon dress aside. It was a definite. I planned to wear it to dinner. She offered to let me borrow it and the others but I wouldn't hear of it. I'd borrowed items before and always worried that I'd spill something on them and because of that I always did.

'No, I'd like to buy the lemon dress, the blue, and the white and silvery dress. I've done well making a profit this past month so this is my treat to myself.' Along with the things I'd bought from Ewan's shop and the wool from Agnes. But that would be all I'd spend on frivolous things for the rest of the summer, probably. These dresses would see me through any parties for the next few seasons, maybe longer. I couldn't imagine ever parting with the lemon chiffon dress.

I insisted on buying them for the fair price that they were but Delphine gave me a discount and put the two dresses in a bag while I slipped the lemon dress back on.

Delphine eyed me carefully when I emerged from the changing room. 'The shoes are great with the dress but...'

'But what?'

'Your hair is one of your top assets. The chignon is nice but if I were you I'd let my hair down. It'll look lovely with the dress, less formal.'

I unclipped my hair and let it fall around my shoulders. I ran a brush through it. I looked at myself in the changing room mirror. She was right. It looked so much better.

I heard Delphine check through the many strings of beaded necklaces in the shop. She picked out a string of crystals and a floral diamante brooch. We both agreed that the necklace was overkill and that the dress didn't need it, however, the diamante flower brooch was perfect.

'Your handbag is too bulky,' she said. 'Here, try this velvet pumpkin bag.' She handed me an amber coloured evening bag that again enhanced the dress without looking like I'd tried too hard.

There was still an hour until dinner and we were chatting about her new collection when my phone rang. It was Ewan.

'Are you ready?'

'I thought you were picking me up at eight.'

'I'm impatient. Besides, it's forecast to be one of the hottest nights of the year. Then it'll probably turn to grey days and rain, so I thought we'd make the most of it and do something before dinner.'

He wanted to come round right away. 'I'm not at home. I'm at Delphine's tea dress shop.'

'I know where that is. I'll be there soon. Wait for me there.'

'I wonder what he has planned?' I said to Delphine.

She shrugged and then said, 'Maybe he's going to take you to the funfair. They've got one of those large wheel types of rides set up in a park near here and a helter skelter. And how appropriate, especially in that dress.'

'Why is that?'

'I think of it as a helter skelter dress because of the cut of the fabric and the design of the gold sparkly threads that wind their way around and down the length of the dress.'

'There's no way I'm going down a helter skelter in this dress.'

'Why not? In years gone by women did all sorts of adventurous things in their tea dresses. Going down a fancy slide won't do it any harm.'

'What about me? The dress might be okay, but will I survive whizzing down it? I haven't done that since I was a wee girl, and even then I screamed all the way.'

Delphine laughed. 'That's the joy of the fair, to be daring and adventurous. You've let your hair down, literally, so let yourself enjoy a bit of light–hearted fun. I know I would.'

By the time she'd convinced me to throw sensibility to the wind, Ewan drove up. He peeped the horn. Delphine gave me a giggling hug and I hurried out into the night in my new dress, hair flowing freely, carrying my pumpkin bag and looking forward to whatever exciting plans Ewan had in mind.

I left my car parked outside her shop, having stashed my purchases and unsuitable handbag in the boot.

I got into Ewan's car and we headed off. Delphine had guessed right. Ewan thought we should walk around the funfair before having dinner. I didn't tell him I was wearing a helter skelter dress. Maybe I'd get away with meandering round with him and admiring everyone else doing the daring stuff.

But Ewan had other plans, including a ride on the wheel that promised a fantastic view of the city.

I took a deep breath and climbed into the seat, making sure that I had a tight grip on Ewan's muscular arm. He was happy to hold on to me, wrapping me securely in his strong embrace while we began to soar towards the top of the ride.

I didn't scream. I sometimes held my breath because the view of the city and all the lights around us for miles was fantastic. The air was hot, even at that height. The forecast was correct. It was one of those scorching summer evenings when everything felt clear and the night air was filled with energy.

'This is wonderful,' I said to him. I couldn't stop smiling.

Ewan leaned close and whispered in my ear. 'You look wonderful too. You're the most beautiful woman here, so I'd better be careful.'

I glanced at him.

'You should know that you have several loyal friends, Tilsie. Agnes, Lisa and two other women from the knitting bee phoned me earlier to warn me.'

'About what?'

'That I shouldn't dare break your heart or do anything to cause you heartache.'

My heart squeezed at the thought that they'd stuck up for me like that. Such sweethearts.

'Well then,' I said to him. 'I hope you take their warning.'

'I do. They said that if I upset you, they'd knit unmentionable parts of my anatomy into woolly pom poms.'

'Sounds like a pertinent threat to me.'

'It is. So I'll be careful not to step out of line tonight, even though I'd love to kiss the breath from you.'

'I'm sure that if you check the small print under their threats you'll see that there's an allowance for kissing, especially at this height.'

He leaned closer and pressed his firm, sensual lips against mine, making me melt into him. For a moment while he kissed me, high above the city, with the night air brushing against my bare legs and through the sheer chiffon of my dress, I let go of all my worries and stress and did what I'd been advised to by Agnes and Delphine — to enjoy my date with this handsome man.

Chapter Seven

Christmas Yarn & Needlework

We wandered around the stalls but we didn't go on the helter–skelter. But I did stand and admire it, remembering when I was a girl that I loved to whiz down and around the traditional funfair rides.

'There's a stand selling candyfloss,' I said. 'I haven't had a pink candyfloss in years. Shall we?' I smiled at him, never thinking he'd scupper my suggestion by being sensible.

'It'll ruin our appetite for dinner.'

True, and yet...would one sweet and light candyfloss really take the edge of our appetites? Not mine I thought, but I didn't push the idea further.

'Shall we head to the restaurant?' he said, scooping me away from the colourful lights and back to where he'd parked the car. 'I've booked our table for dinner.'

We drove through the city and along Princes Street which was aglow with lights and traffic. There was always something magical about this street and all the little niches surrounding it. And the shops. I loved the shops. On evenings like this the shop windows seemed to shine as if they'd had an extra polish. Couples, linking arms, walked along Princes Street, and I wished we could've done that. How many scorching hot evenings like this would there be before the bite of autumn? I often felt I was letting so many things slip by without enjoying them.

Then I glanced over at Ewan and realised I had a whole evening of his company ahead of me. My stomach fluttered with excitement. I couldn't remember the last time I'd felt like that.

We were seated at our table in the restaurant. Everything about it was classy. Ewan had put the jacket of his suit on and straightened his tie. Everyone was well–dressed and well–behaved.

Our table was beside one of the windows with a magnificent view of the city. A river of traffic flowed below us and filtered off into the distance. The outlines of the spires, the ancient architecture, were highlighted against the night sky that refused to be completely dark, as if it too was making the most of this languid evening.

Our meal consisted of numerous small courses of the finest cuisine. No lavish ice cream confections tonight.

We chatted about our work mainly, and I suppose it was the only thing that marred the perfect evening. But what else did we have to discuss? Two business people who were involved in work that had brought us together were bound to talk shop. I wasn't into any sports and Ewan had nothing to say about his sporting past that I didn't already know from his website. We were far more enthusiastic about discussing the new trends in home decor and what was due to be popular in the autumn and winter.

'I love my new duvet cover,' I told him, detailing how it felt, then wished I hadn't painted such a vivid picture of being in bed with the windows open. I didn't want him to think I was trying to entice him. I wasn't.

'I can't remember the last time we've had such a scorching summer,' he said. 'I lay on top of my bed and couldn't sleep for the heat. But this time next week it could be cold and rainy so I won't dare complain.'

'I don't mind the rain. There's something cosy about it.'

He smiled at me. 'I like that about you.'

'What?'

'You like the simple things and appreciate them. I noticed that when you were at the house.'

'You do have a lovely house. You're very fortunate.'

'I never thought I'd stay there for as long. I always intended living abroad or at least travelling around Europe and America, especially New York. I'd love to live there.'

'I thought you said you couldn't imagine living anywhere else other than the coach house.'

'In Edinburgh, yes. I'd rather live there than the city centre again, but I'm hoping to travel to New York for a few weeks in the autumn.'

'Really? What about your shop? Would you hire your friend, the businessman you mentioned, to keep an eye on it?'

He nodded.

He'd done it again, made me feel disappointed and yet I had no right to. This was our first dinner, a first date.

'If I go, and I'm still considering it, I'd be back within six weeks, two months at the most. We'd still be able to see each other.'

He made me feel like I was the possessive type and I shuddered at the thought. I wasn't that type at all, yet it seemed reasonable to feel surprised to learn on our first date that he was planning to leave and not come back for months.

I smiled and tried not to look perturbed.

'That really is a beautiful dress you're wearing.'

'It's from Delphine's shop, from her fairytale collection of vintage dresses.'

He looked over at me. 'Beautiful, really beautiful.'

I think he was meaning me and not just the dress. I felt my cheeks flush with warmth.

He spoke in a deep, sensual tone so no one, except me, could hear him. 'Without wanting to risk the wrath of the knitting bee ladies, do you think there's a chance for us? Would you take a chance on getting involved with a man like me?'

'A man like you? You mean a man who doesn't want a permanent relationship? A man who doesn't even like the mention of marriage? Frankly, I think it's a bit early in the game to discuss our future.'

'I know what I said about marriage, and I do feel that way, but it doesn't mean I don't want a proper relationship, one that will last. I do. I'm just not the marrying kind.'

'I understand.'

'Do you?'

'I understand more than you think I do.'

We were quiet for a few moments and I gazed out at the lights of the city, watching the traffic flow throughout the streets.

'Can we go back to how we felt earlier at the funfair?' he said.

I wanted that too. The atmosphere had become heavy. 'I'd like that. And let's forget about work, and marketing strategies and new ranges of linen bedding.'

'Don't diss the bedding, especially as you've yet to try the new linen sheets. If you thought the duvet felt great against your naked skin, wait until you feel these sheets.'

'I didn't say I was naked,' I said lightly.

He gave me a sexy grin. 'You implied it, and painted quite an attractive picture in my mind.'

We continued to tease and joke with each other, and I was glad the atmosphere had lifted again. Maybe Ewan was just a summer fling, but so what? Perhaps we would become deeply involved and I'd be torn apart when the summer was over, if he left to travel abroad. But there was no guarantee that I would. Love and romance and making the right decisions all the time wasn't guaranteed either. He was a sexy, handsome man, and I wanted some romance in my life. Everyone had expected my ex would ask me to marry him, and we'd get engaged and settle down, and look how that ended in a pile of heartache just because I wanted my own business. Ewan didn't have a problem with my career. Every relationship had it's good and bad points.

I was still mentally arguing with myself, or trying to convince myself that I could do what I wanted and to hell with the outcome, when Ewan suggested we head back to his house — for coffee.

'Coffee, huh?'

He nodded and smiled.

'We don't drink coffee, Ewan.'

'We'll have to find something else to do then, won't we?'

I didn't imagine it would involve picking brambles in the moonlight and giggling like a couple of fools as Ewan tripped over the lawn and almost dropped our punnet of fruit.

On the drive to his house we'd chatted again about his plans to go to New York but he dismissed them lightly. 'It's just an idea. I probably won't do it.'

I'd also told him I wasn't the type to jump into bed on a first date, and he seemed okay with that. He told me he didn't want our evening to end at the restaurant and was happy to enjoy my company at his house without wrinkling the linen sheets on his bed.

I never set foot in his bedroom, though we did kiss for ages, snuggled up together on the sofa. And there were a few stolen hugs and kisses in the kitchen while we made tea.

Then he drove me back to pick up my car at Delphine's shop. She'd gone home and the shop was in darkness except for the fairy lights in the window. She'd pinned up a dress where Hetty had been and the lights made it glitter like stardust.

Ewan gave me a lingering goodnight kiss before I got into my car and drove off.

No sleep for me that night. I was far too excited about everything and sat up in bed with my laptop and did a ton of work.

I finally closed the laptop and had two hours sleep before my alarm went off. Unlike the previous mornings, I woke refreshed and bouncing with energy. It was amazing what an evening of sizzling hot kisses and a trip to the funfair could do to boost my energy levels.

I went to Agnes' shop later that morning. I wanted to see what she'd done with the new shop. It looked fantastic. I waved to her through the window as I approached the shop and gave her the thumbs up.

I went inside. The shop wasn't open to customers until the photographs had been taken.

'The photographer is due soon,' said Agnes. 'I've been up most of the night getting the shop ready. Hetty sets off the new window display beautifully.'

The original shop was all neat and tidy and packed full of yarn and needlework accessories, but through the adjoining doorway, the vintage–theme shop looked amazing.

Agnes had extended her haberdashery. It suited the theme of the shop. Satin and velvet ribbons, buttons galore, embroidery floss and various types of thread were arranged to entice knitters and sewists.

The shelves were piled with yarn and fat quarters of fabric, along with bolts of material including silky lining from the palest oyster and shell pink to fabulous emerald, sapphire and royal blue.

An antique bread basket was brimming with balls of wool, and she'd used floral teacups and teapots to add to the old–fashioned theme. At the doorway sat a little post–box for customers to post letters to Santa. 'I've included the post–box because I thought it went with the vintage theme and the Christmas corner of the shop,' said Agnes. 'I've used it in my shop for the past few years at Christmastime and customers like it. No doubt it'll fill up with cheerful notes and letters. Matt likes to drop a letter in. It's just a wee bit of frivolity. Last year he scribbled a note saying he wanted an Aran knit jumper so I knitted one for him. Dear knows what he'll ask for this year.'

The new shop was stocked with Christmas yarn too, but she'd even given this a traditional look by hanging up strings of little lantern fairy lights.

'The lights are years old but they still work,' said Agnes, taking me over to have a look at them. The colours of the lanterns were rich and gave a warm glow to the Christmas display.

Knitted Christmas baubles were draped along the edges of the shelves like festive bunting and she'd pinned up the patterns to make them.

Knitting dollies were lined up beside the embroidery threads and knitting needles, bringing back memories of having used a little wooden dolly years ago to knit cords for handbags and bracelets.

Agnes had used an old set of drawers to drape trims, bunting and pom poms, and to display knitting needle bags, crochet hooks and a selection of knitting and needlework patterns.

At the opposite side of the shop, Hetty stood in the window with her silvery–grey chiffon dress glistening in the sunlight.

A car pulled up outside. 'Here's the photographer,' said Agnes. She fluffed her hair, adjusted her spectacles and smoothed the skirt she was wearing along with a pretty broderie anglaise blouse. 'How do I look?'

'Fantastic and so does the shop.'

I waited with her while the photographer, who was the son of one of the knitting bee ladies and a professional photographer, took numerous pictures. I helped move Hetty so that she was included in various shots of the old–fashioned haberdashery. I even changed her dress. The tea rose dress suited being part of the photographs near the Christmas display and were perfect for shots with the teacups and teapots.

After the photographer left, Agnes opened the shop to customers. Lots had turned up to see the new vintage selection. I didn't have any meetings scheduled so I stayed until after lunchtime. During snatched moments I told her about my dinner date with Ewan.

'Is he a good kisser?' she asked me, so loud that some of the customers overheard.

'Ssh! Who said I kissed him?'

'Of course you kissed him, Tilsie. You've got that first flush of romance look to you. The type of glow you get when you've had a romantic evening.' She gave me a knowing look.

I held my hands up. 'I didn't get up to anything scandalous.'

'But you snogged the face off Ewan, didn't you?' said Agnes while serving a customer.

The customer gasped. 'You kissed Ewan? Big, handsome Ewan?'

Agnes nodded firmly.

The woman grinned at me. 'Lucky you. He's gorgeous.'

While they continued to discuss this, a text message came through on my phone. I read it. It was from Ewan: *I had a great time last night, Tilsie. I'm going to do the trip that I talked about. I'm off to New York. It'll be great to see you when I get back.*

I sat there for a few moments before Agnes said to me, 'Are you okay?'

The flush had gone from my cheeks.

I'd been on a high from kissing Ewan and having had a wonderful evening. Then on a low getting the text message. It was just my luck that I'd had no romance for a couple of years, and then after my first date he'd run off to New York.

I held up my phone and let Agnes read the message.

I watched the anger flare up across her cheeks as she read it.

'I'm not going to wait for him,' I told her.

She pursed her lips with rage, grabbed my phone and called Ewan. He answered, thinking it was me. I heard the surprise in his tone when he realised it was Agnes.

Her message to him was succinct. 'Pom poms, Ewan, pom poms.'

'I get what you mean, Agnes,' he said. 'But I've a flight to catch. I have to run.'

'You'd better run, Ewan. You'd better run,' she shouted down the phone at him and then clicked off.

She handed the phone back gently and gave me a caring look. 'I'm sorry, Tilsie. Men are rotten, selfish bastards.'

Matt walked in. 'Not all men.'

Her tone softened. 'No, you're okay, Matt. You've been very helpful to me. I appreciate it.' She turned to me. 'Matt came in early this morning before opening his shop to move the heavy counter again where I needed it and helped me shift all my stock around.'

Matt had a note in his hand, a piece of paper carefully folded. The atmosphere in the shop was sizzling with our anger and upset. 'I came to post my letter to Santa, but I sense I've called at an inconvenient time.' He looked at me but I didn't feel like starting to explain the dilemma.

Agnes blurted out what had happened.

Matt shook his head at me. 'If I'd known you were thinking of going on a date with Ewan I'd have tried to talk you out of it because I knew he was leaving to go to New York.'

'You knew?' I said.

'Ewan's been in my shop buying outdoor adventure clothes for his trip abroad. He was in last week. That's what I'd popped into the knitting bee on Wednesday night to tell Agnes. I thought it was just a bit of gossip and forgot about it when I was introduced to Tilsie and had my bum insulted. It didn't seem important.'

Agnes' shoulders slumped and her voice lost its anger. 'If only we'd known.'

Matt sensed it was better to leave, but before he went he said to us, 'Why is it that decent men like myself are overlooked in favour of chocolate box handsome shite bags?' He posted his letter in the post–box, and then he left. He'd come over with his letter as a bit of a joke and I felt bad that it had fallen flat.

We were all quiet for a moment and then I said, 'I wish I did fancy Matt, but I don't.'

'I fancy him,' one of the customers said. 'And so does my friend, Fay. She's one of your knitting bee girls.'

'Fay? She's a dancer, isn't she?' said Agnes. 'Lovely young woman.' She paused and then said to the customer, 'And she really likes Matt? Not that there's any reason for her not to.'

'Fancies the pants off of him. Have you seen him lately? Once he shifted the weight off his arse, she's been hinting that she'd love to date him if he asked her.'

'She should ask him,' I said.

'She's too shy,' the customer explained. 'She's used to men asking her out.'

'Fay's a looker,' said Agnes. 'I'm sure she has plenty of offers.'

The customer nodded. 'She does, but she's not the flirty type. Fay wants a proper relationship and to settle down.'

Agnes unlocked the post–box. 'I wonder what Matt wants from Santa this Christmas.' She unfolded his letter and read it aloud. 'Dear Santa, could I please have a girlfriend for Christmas? Someone who would want to marry me eventually would be extra nice. Failing that, a jumper would be great.' She put the letter back in the box and locked it again.

Agnes sighed. 'I wouldn't usually try to be a matchmaker but I'll make an exception for Matt and Fay.'

'I'll help,' I offered.

Although I was still cut to the core about Ewan, I felt a bit better knowing that Agnes had threatened to knit his unmentionables into pom poms.

'Count me in,' said Fay's friend.

Another customer smiled over at us. 'Count me in as well,' she said.

Santa tumbled from his grotto almost taking the fairy lanterns with him. Agnes lifted him up. 'And you can keep out of it. You and your squeaker are nothing but trouble.'

Chapter Eight

Christmas Knitting

I sat on the back step of my house knitting the snowman. I'd made myself an easy dinner, eating it in the kitchen with the back door open, then settled down to knit him. The evening was hot and the sun cast a summery glow across the sky making everything in my garden look lovely. It wasn't a patch on Ewan's garden but the lawn looked tidy and the flowers put on a colourful display, dependable as ever, even though I hadn't had much time to bother with them.

Far more dependable than men, I grumbled to myself, then immediately discarded the thought. I wasn't going to become bitter because of the likes of Ewan. No way. One rotten date was not going to taint everything.

I continued knitting while thinking things over...

I'd taken a chance on dating Ewan and it hadn't paid off. However, I now had three beautiful dresses hanging in my wardrobe and a pumpkin bag. I increased the number of stitches on my needles and forged on with the pattern. It was an easy thing to knit and just right for pondering the pros and cons of what had happened between Ewan and me.

Apart from stopping for cups of tea, I knitted the snowman until I'd finished him. The night had deepened, and I worked by the beam from the wall light outside the kitchen door that came on automatically when it was dark.

The white yarn sparkled under the lamplight. I'd yet to knit his hat and scarf, but the snowman himself was knitted and stuffed and I'd stitched a cheery face on him with yarn.

I tidied my knitting away and got ready for bed. Things felt better, and I was more settled in my own thoughts. And things always looked brighter in the morning.

I drove past Ewan's shop the following day. The shop was open and I caught a glimpse of a mature gentleman behind the counter.

I parked outside Agnes' shop and heard her chatting with Lisa and a couple of other ladies as I walked in.

'I'm glad you're here, Tilsie,' said Agnes. She held up a small envelope that looked like it had been made by hand from white craft paper. 'We've got a letter for Matt. I've phoned and asked him to come over.'

Lisa smiled kindly at me and whispered. 'I heard about Ewan. Are you okay?'

'Yes, thanks, Lisa. I'm fine.'

'Men are shites,' she said as Matt came into the shop.

'I think that's all you women talk about — knitting and men,' he said.

Agnes adjusted her spectacles and stared at him. 'Is there a problem with that?'

'Nooo, it's fine by me,' he said.

There's was a moment's lull. I didn't know what was in the envelope but I guessed it was part of the matchmaking plan to get him together with Fay.

'You wanted me to come over?' he said, prompting Agnes to explain.

'Yes, a letter arrived for you this morning,' she began.

He jumped to the wrong conclusion that the local postie had mixed up the mail.

'No, Matt,' said Agnes. 'The letter's from Santa.'

He let out a guffaw as he accepted the little envelope. 'Oh very funny, ladies. A letter for me from Santa. That was a quick reply all the way from the North Pole. Did he have the elves working overtime to help him deal with it?' He turned the envelope over in his hands, happy to go along with the joke, but wondering whether he should open it or not. Had we put something inside that was going to jump out at him? 'You lot are up to something,' he said. He looked at me.

'I'd open it if I were you, Matt.'

Trusting me, he carefully opened the envelope and read the letter. His eyes blinked as he read it again. He looked at us. 'Is this for real?'

Agnes nodded and smiled at him. 'She's liked you for a while, but was too shy to tell you. If you ask her out I'm sure she'll say yes.'

If ever a man looked like he wanted to make a phone call immediately.

We all got an excited kiss on the cheek. I may have received two. It was difficult to tell as Matt whirled around.

'Thank you, Agnes. Thanks, Tilsie, Lisa and I'm sorry I don't know all your names ladies, but thanks.' He went to hurry out and then shouted over his shoulder, 'And thank you Santa.'

'I think that went well,' Agnes mused.

'Hmm,' I said.

And then we all laughed and cheered.

Sometimes meddling did pay off. Matt would have a girlfriend well before Christmas. A summer romance for him was a sure thing.

I didn't hit the romantic jackpot that summer, but I considered myself lucky that my marketing business was thriving without draining all my spare time. I had time to enjoy my knitting. I often went along to the Wednesday night knitting bee and I'd made some great friends there as well as two jumpers, a short–sleeved top and a knitted skirt — the first I'd ever made. Knitted in a figure–hugging rib pattern, the sea grey skirt cut just above the knee and was so easy to wear. I wore it to a couple of business meetings and knew I'd get a lot of wear out of it on colder days, teaming it with woollen tights and boots. I planned to knit another one in shades of midnight blue using one of the luxury yarns that Agnes had ordered in for the autumn.

The more I knitted the more I loved it. Being part of the knitting bee provided constant inspiration. One of the women had knitted a wedding dress for her niece using the finest yarn and it was more like a work of fairytale art. It got featured in a magazine and this brought even more attention to our knitting bee and Agnes' shop.

As the summer wore on, the heat dwindled, but I wasn't sad when it rained. As I'd told Ewan, I loved the rain and enjoyed cosy evenings snuggled on the sofa listening to it hit off the windows, safe inside my house.

Ewan had remained in New York, leaving his friend to run the shop. Agnes kept us up–to–date with the gossip. I didn't go back to Ewan's shop even though he was on the other side of the Atlantic. I hadn't heard from him and I didn't want to. Not in a petulant way, but because I felt no good would come from raking over the past, a past that had barely existed. Moping around wasn't my style. Never had been. Never would be.

The autumn was one of the most beautiful in years. The hot summer, followed by fresh rainy days, had made the trees lush with greenery and the parks around the city had never looked so verdant.

The tree–lined street where Agnes' shop was situated mellowed from warm bronze to burnished copper as the weeks went on. Edinburgh was such a beautiful city that wore each season well. The streets weren't paved with gold, but in the autumn the trees cast it in every gold hue you could wish for with their scattered leaves.

Agnes' feature in the newspaper for the launch of her new shop had brought plenty of new customers, but since then there had been a steady increase in trade and her vintage yarns and haberdashery was thriving. The Christmas yarns and needlework accessories were particularly popular and she'd had to restock regularly to keep up with demand.

Online orders had also picked up, but customers from near and far enjoyed visiting the actual shop to experience the vintage feel of it. A knitting bee on the West Coast of Scotland, organised by a Mrs Bramble, made the trip across to Edinburgh some weekends just to browse and buy yarn for their knitting bee projects. This was what I'd been hoping for — customer loyalty, knitting and sewing enthusiasts who appreciated the fine selection that Agnes' shop offered them. At the heart of it all, it really came down to her ability to trawl through the vast choices of yarns and patterns and choose what would be popular with customers.

At six o'clock one evening as I finished work I walked from the Rose Street area and then down to Princes Street to unwind after a busy week and to window shop.

Princes Street looked like it has been gilded in the fading autumn light, and with the gleaming reflections from the windows, I blinked twice, thinking my eyes were playing tricks on me. Was that Stewarton looking at me from across the street? I held my hand up to shield my eyes for a better look. Was it? I hadn't seen him since...I tried not to think of the last time when I'd blamed Santa for breaking wind. I knew Stewarton didn't believe me and I still squirmed with embarrassment at the memory.

The man across the street wore a dark grey suit and a familiar handsome expression. Traffic drove past, separating us. The traffic was always busy this time of night when people were heading home

75

from work or into the city for dinner, to go for a drink in the numerous bars and restaurants, or take in a show at the theatres.

I craned to see the man but I wasn't tall enough to peer over some of the cars, and when the buses went by I had to wait until they'd gone before focussing again on the tall, broad–shoulder figure so near and yet so far.

The traffic lights finally turned to red and the traffic ground to a halt. I went to step off the pavement when someone brushed against me in her haste to run across the road.

Julie? I'd recognise those heels and scrawny arse anywhere. Then I remembered. Of course, I was standing outside the department store where she'd opened her pop–up shop weeks ago. I'd read the feature in the newspaper. I'd resisted having a nosey at her fashion boutique within the store. Okay, so I'd had one peck the week it opened from across the carousels of clothes and rails dripping with dresses in the department store, making sure that Julie didn't see me. I thought her shop looked pretty impressive but gave a lot of the credit to Stewarton who no doubt had arranged everything. Maybe not the clothes, but everything else, including the finances, advertising and promotion of her venture. She also had a shop assistant. All Julie had to do was strut around looking fashionably dressed and important. No stretch there I thought.

I blinked back to concentrating on the busy street. Julie had made it across the road. The traffic was waiting for the green light and I could see her run up to Stewarton her arms flapping as she probably complained about something being less than perfect in her world.

I noticed there was no show of affection. They looked like two business acquaintances who were off to a dinner meeting, both well–dressed and with a sense of urgency to their lives.

Julie never knew I saw her, but Stewarton did. For a second, our eyes connected across the stream of traffic as the lights signalled the cars to drive on. He nodded acknowledgment. I did the same. Nothing in his expression, as when I'd first met him, gave me any hint of his thoughts.

The traffic picked up speed and within moments we were separated again. I saw the briefest glimpse of them as they walked away towards an area where cars were parked. I assumed he'd continued to be loyal and had come to pick her up after she'd finished working at the pop–up shop. Loyal to the last. That was Stewarton. I couldn't fault him on that.

I popped into Delphine's Fairytale Tea Dress shop on the way back, not on business, she didn't need any marketing as her shop was thriving and she'd have been unable to deal with any more orders for her fabulous dresses and accessories. No, I dropped by for tea and a chat.

Hetty was back in the window display. Autumn fashions adorned the window and Hetty's dress of chiffon and organza had short sleeves shaped like leaves. Gold and bronze beading sparkled on the sleeves and reminded me of the top that I'd been making at the knitting bee. Agnes had patterns for the leaves and we'd all been making them as brooches, handbag accessories and even sewn on to the altered sleeves of plain T–shirts to create something that looked unique.

Vintage–style bracelets hung from an art deco figurine. I bought an amber and gold–coloured beaded bracelet sewn on to satin ribbon and fastened with an oyster clasp. 'It'll suit the short–sleeved top I knitted. I love the shades of autumn.'

Delphine smiled and gazed out the shop window. 'Me too, and the city is looking really gilded this year. I thought I'd dress up Hetty to match it.' She turned her attention back to me. 'Have you heard anything from Ewan or shouldn't I ask? Perhaps you've tried to forget about him.'

'From the snippets of gossip gathered from the knitting bee we've heard that he extended his trip in New York because another restaurant client wanted him to advise on their table linen and decor. The owner asked Ewan to help with other restaurants and boutique hotels. He's supposed to be coming back in October but I won't be holding my breath.'

'Finished with him?'

'Totally.'

'What if he comes back and realises he made a mistake and has missed you all these weeks he's been away? Men can be such silly creatures. I'm not trying to influence you, Tilsie, but you seemed to really like him that evening you went out to dinner.'

'People can make mistakes, but I'm glad I didn't get to know him better, especially when I went home with him that night.' I hinted that he'd wanted me to spend the night with him, an intimate night.

'Love's so difficult, isn't it?'

'I've been simplifying things. Work, knitting, enjoying chatting with the knitting bee girls. Making time for my knitting, my house and garden. When romance comes along, I'll take things easy.'

'Sounds like a sensible plan.'

Delphine brought a box out from under the counter. 'If you see Agnes will you give her these?' She ran her hands through the selection of vintage buttons and trims in the box. 'I got a load of these from a wholesaler friend in London. I'll never use them all without doubling up on the designs and I try to make most of my dresses one–offs. I thought Agnes could use them, maybe even for the knitting bee.' She scooped up a handful of the buttons. 'These were popular on jumpers in the 1940s. Knitters would sew them on to jumpers to jazz up the designs. The buttons didn't do anything. They were used as brooches.'

'We've been knitting brooches with diamante.'

'Well, I hope the girls can make use of them.'

'Thanks, Delphine. You'll have to pop along to the knitting bee some night.'

'Yes, I think I'll do that. It's Wednesday nights?'

I nodded, and hoped I'd see her there soon.

Agnes poured the buttons into a classic sweetie jar and sat it on the shop counter. 'I'll let customers help themselves to a button or two and the knitting bee girls can use as many as they want.'

She tied the lace trims into little bundles and put them in a basket beside the sweetie jar.

'Delphine says she might come along to the knitting bee,' I said.

'I hope she does. I think she'd enjoy it, and she could catch up on all the gossip.'

'She was asking about Ewan and I told her he's not due back until October. She was wondering if I'd forgive him and start dating him again.'

'After what he did?' Her voice was high pitched.

'I told her I was finished with Ewan.' I sat down on the quilted chair beside the counter.

Agnes continued to arrange the displays. 'Is there something you're not telling me?'

I blinked up at her.

She tilted her head and said, 'Well, is there?'

I sighed. 'I saw Stewarton in Princes Street with Julie.'

Agnes pursed her lips. 'So he's still with her.'

'She didn't see me, but he looked across the street at me and then he was gone again with her.'

'Did he wave over at you? Did he smile?'

'No, but we saw each other and I felt...I don't know...'

'Like you were looking at the one that got away?'

'Seems silly, especially as we hardly knew each other. But that night at dinner, I saw a different side to him.' I smiled to myself, remembering his face when he saw the ice cream served up and how we'd laughed that evening. The memory still lingered with me and he'd crossed my mind a few times during the past months.

Agnes sat down and picked up her knitting. She was knitting a Christmas jumper in sparkly red yarn. Her festive jumper patterns with matching bobble hats were selling well and she knitted samples to display in the shop to show customers what type of yarns suited the Christmassy designs. This one had a reindeer and a Santa on it. Although it was a novelty design I loved the traditional red, green and gold colours of the jumper. 'I'm surprised he's still with Julie.'

I sighed. 'I guess they're better suited than we thought. Even he thought they were heading for a split. Sometimes the couples you never think will last stick together.'

'Matt and Fay are going strong. I'd never have thought Fay fancied Matt.'

'That's been a while now they've been going out.'

'The time's flying in. It'll be Hallowe'en soon. We'll have to start knitting acorns, hazelnuts and spider webs for the window display.' She pulled out a list from under the counter. 'Lisa is knitting three pumpkins.' She checked further down the list. 'I can't remember who is knitting the cauldron.' She held up the list of Hallowe'en items that the knitting bee made for the annual display.

'Put me down for the acorns.'

'I've got gorgeous metallic gold yarn for the tops of the acorns this year. Knits up like a dream. I'm going to knit some spider webs with it to show how it would work well for a lace–knit shrug.' She took her phone from her knitting bag. 'I'm also knitting a black cat. I've got a great vintage pattern but I'm using Cookie as inspiration, especially for the face.' She held the phone up to show me a photograph of Cookie. 'I snapped this pic of him the other day when he was in my garden.'

'Look at him now.' The fluffy little kitten had grown into a fair–sized young cat.

Agnes flicked the phone off. 'Like I said, the time is flying by. You don't realise until you see things like Cookie. From a wee bundle of fluff to a sturdy young cat.'

'Does he still snore?'

'Oh yes, but I love him to bits. My house is his second home. He's always padding in when I have my kitchen door open. He's old enough now to go out on the prowl and to be left in the house by himself, so I don't need to cat sit him these days, but he's in the garden every day and I get to share him with my neighbour.'

She held up the pattern for the knitted black cat.

'The resemblance is uncanny,' I said, smiling.

'Cookie's got a fluffier tail, but I'll soon fluff up the yarn after I've knitted it with a teasel brush. I thought I'd add some of that midnight blue wool in with the black to add depth to the colour and the texture.'

'The new wool has arrived?'

'Yes, and I've put some aside for that skirt you wanted to make.'

When I knitted my first acorn I found it a bit fiddly and it took me almost half an hour to get it right. By my twentieth acorn — my contribution to Agnes' Hallowe'en display, I had the technique down to around ten minutes.

Although it was fantastic to knit items that I would actually wear, there was something satisfying about coming home after an arduous day's work, with my mind buzzing with the marketing strategies I had to create for my clients, and knitting something I could finish in an evening.

One night I knitted a pumpkin using the spare gold metallic yarn left over from the acorns. I followed Lisa's pattern and it turned out a treat. I sat the gold pumpkin on the window ledge of the living room. When the autumn sun was out it glowed as if it was alight.

Simple pleasures, I told myself, were often better than wild nights out, though I'd had a few party nights at the knitting shop. The knitting bee provided the right amount of social life while I was busy with my work. I rarely missed a Wednesday night at the bee and I shuddered to think what my life would've been like without it. Far emptier and less enriched that's for sure.

I especially liked that I could relax and didn't have to watch my back when I was there, something I hadn't quite forgotten from the cut–throat, corporate world I'd come from. Often I didn't know who my friends were in that fierce arena, but at the knitting bee no one had time for fractious nonsense. If one member knitted a wonderful jumper using an intricate pattern, we were happy that she had the higher level skills to make it. We didn't vie against each other. There was none of that. Beginner knitters were welcome, though they soon caught the knitting bug and with encouragement from experienced bee members they weren't novices for long.

Years from now I was sure I'd remember the knitting bee as the time I made everything from an acorn to a skirt and relaxed and laughed during the Wednesday evenings in likeminded company.

The Hallowe'en party was fun, with lanterns strung across the shop window and knitted spider webs. Agnes had sold the pumpkins that Lisa had knitted, and my acorns and numerous other novelty items, well before the party. Customers had snapped them up along with patterns and yarn to knit some themselves.

The cake shop nearby made sticky toffee apple cake and treacle scones that we scoffed with copious amounts of tea and coffee.

It was one of the happiest Hallowe'en nights I'd had in years. Matt won first prize for his fancy dress outfit. He'd come as a mountaineer. Agnes gave him first prize for originality, hoping he'd get the joke, but he was delighted he'd won and left with a stuffed black cat softie.

Chapter Nine

The Chocolatier's Tearoom

November announced its arrival in a flurry of icy rain. The hot summer days and mellow autumn were a distant memory — as was Ewan. He didn't come back in late October as we'd heard and missed our Hallowe'en party at the knitting shop. It was a shame really because Agnes threatened to boil up his woolly pom poms in the knitted cauldron.

She wasn't harbouring resentment from what he'd done to me. She was annoyed with him for leaving his shop for so long. Okay, so it was his business and he could do what he wanted, but as the weeks went on, it started to impact other shops in the street, particularly Agnes' shop.

'His customers keep coming in and asking me where he is and when he's coming back,' Agnes grumbled. 'It's not their fault and I'm not going to snap at them, but really...Ewan needs a sign up in his front window explaining things instead of it being the responsibility of other shopkeepers. Normally, I wouldn't mind, but this is going on for ages.'

'Did you ask the man who is running Ewan's shop to put a notice up?' She'd told me she was going to.

'I did, but he said that Ewan didn't want a sign in the window and neither did he. He said it could adversely affect sales if customers stopped to read it and thought that they'd wait until Ewan came back before going in to buy stuff. He said they'd lose out on sales.' She took her spectacles off, something I noticed she did when she was angry and flustered. 'I know they've got a point, but it's not right. All the wee shops in this part of the street come and go with each other. Business is hard for everyone these days. I'm fortunate that mine is doing well, but Ewan is being a selfish prat.'

I tried to shield myself with my umbrella and hurried along the street in the lashing rain when Stewarton phoned.

I dashed into a shop doorway and took the call. The traffic swished by and I had to ask him to speak up so I could hear him.

'I said,' he repeated, 'are you interested in speaking at the convention this month? We spoke about it at the restaurant in the summer.'

'I eh...' He'd taken me off–guard. I'd been shopping after a hectic week and had treated myself to a vintage coat, a fabulous Mackintosh from a shop that sold preloved clothes. It had been raining all day, for the past two days in fact, and it was a real bargain. I'd seen it in the shop window and had gone in to buy the coat before heading to a meeting at 4:30 p.m. My mind was buzzing with thoughts about the meeting, my new coat and wondering where exactly I'd parked my car. The last thing I expected was a call from Stewarton.

'The payment still stands,' he said, giving me the incentive I needed to agree to take part in the convention. If truth be known, the money would come in handy for Christmas and I could network and make contacts at the convention.

'Yes, I'm interested,' I managed to say as the rain tried to sweep under my umbrella.

'Where are you?' he said. 'You sound like you're standing on the bow of a ship in a storm.'

'Close. I'm in the centre of Edinburgh in the pouring rain, sheltering in a doorway, trying to keep myself and my shopping dry.'

'I'm near the Grassmarket. Tell me where you are and I'll come and get you.'

'No need to send out a rescue party just yet. My car is parked somewhere nearby. I'm on my way to a business meeting so I'll have to go.'

'Wherever you are I could be there in less than ten minutes.'

I looked at the busy traffic. 'Not in this traffic.'

'I am tenacious. Tell me where you are.'

'I have to run, Stewarton. Call me later.'

'Okay.'

I clicked the phone off and, holding tight to my shopping bags and my umbrella, I ran like blazes towards my car.

I shrugged my wet coat off and threw it on the back seat. I turned on the engine, the wipers to full, and headed into the sea of traffic headlights wondering why I felt so elated at hearing from Stewarton.

I finished the meeting and was heading to Agnes' shop when my phone rang.

I parked my car outside her shop.

'Finished your meeting yet?' said Stewarton.

'Yes. It's been a hectic day.'

'Where are you now?'

'Outside Agnes' shop.'

'I could be there in a few minutes. I'd like to chat to you about the convention.'

'We could chat tomorrow. Email me details of the convention.'

'What's wrong with tonight?'

I searched for a reason. Nope, couldn't find one.

He dived into my hesitation with a tempting question. 'Do you like chocolate?'

'Well, yes —'

'I'll buy you tea and chocolate cake at the chocolatier's shop. It's just down the street from Agnes. I'll pick you up at her shop in about twenty minutes.'

He didn't sound as if he was prepared to give up easily so I yielded to temptation. For the chocolate. Not for Stewarton. I wasn't in the least bit tempted by him. Was I?

'Okay,' I agreed. 'See you soon.'

I went to hang up but he called to me, managing to relay his short message before the call ended. 'I split up with Julie.'

The message affected me in a way I didn't expect. It made me feel excited.

Before I could respond he'd gone.

'He's split up with Julie?' Agnes sounded delighted.

'He wants to talk to me about speaking at the convention he's organising later this month.' I checked the time. 'He's picking me up here. He's taking me to the chocolatier's shop for tea and cake. I've never been there.'

'You'll love it. Caelan Broadie is a master chocolatier. Lisa and I treat ourselves to his chocolates every so often.' She pulled a tea cosy that she'd been knitting from one of her bags. Agnes was always knitting something for someone. 'He asked me to knit a chocolate–themed tea cosy for his tearoom display. I thought these two yarns looked like chocolate. What do you think?'

84

She held up a rich chocolate brown and copper–coloured striped cosy. She'd almost finished it. 'I decided to knit it in garter stitch rather than stocking stitch because it gives a fuller texture to the cosy and really makes the yarn glitter.'

'It's so beautiful I'd almost wear it as a hat. Without the gaps for the teapot spout and handle of course. I love the combination of colours.'

She tucked it back into her knitting bag. 'So what are you going to have from the chocolatier's menu? I'd recommend Caelan's chocolate fudge cake. The one with layers of chocolate buttercream and decorated with chocolate cherries. My mouth is watering at the thought of it.'

So was mine. Lunch had been a blur and I hadn't had dinner.

A car pulled up outside.

'Here's Stewarton,' said Agnes, giving me a knowing smile.

'What's that smile for?'

'I sense a bit of romance in the air.'

'Nonsense,' I said sounding totally unconvincing. 'We're just meeting to discuss business. And enjoying chocolate while we're at it.'

She tapped her nose with one of the knitting needles that were an almost permanent fixture in her hands. 'I sense something brewing. And I'm never wrong when it comes to things like that.'

'Ready to go?' said Stewarton.

I picked up my bag and tried not to stare at him. I'd forgotten how handsome he was. Not like Ewan. No, Stewarton wore more deeply on my senses, and I wanted to pause and take him in. He probably wasn't leaner than when I'd last seen him but that's the impression I had when he arrived at the shop. Lean, tall, elegant and moneyed. I wondered what he thought about me. He acknowledged Agnes but it was me he was staring at. Whatever was he thinking? My hair had been soaked twice during the rainy day but somehow I'd tamed it into sitting smooth around the shoulders of my jacket. Inside I felt anything but smooth though I did my utmost to hide it.

At that moment Santa wobbled from the shelf, bounced off the roof of the knitted grotto, did a backflip and landed at Stewarton's feet giving his usual disgruntled noise.

Stewarton's face lit–up with realisation. He glanced at me, then at Santa. I saw the embarrassment cross his face.

Agnes picked Santa up and gave him a firm telling off. 'You keep your opinions about Stewarton to yourself.' She stuffed him on the shelf beside a display of knitted brooches and haberdashery items.

I gave Agnes a nod, letting her know that I'd tell her all about my tea and chocolate date with Stewarton later.

Stewarton led the way to his car. 'It hardly seems worth driving to the chocolatier's shop.'

'Leave the car here. We can walk there in a couple of minutes.' The shop was further down the road and there didn't appear to be many parking spaces so it made sense to walk. The rain had stopped although dark clouds loomed in the early evening sky.

Stewarton escorted me safely across the street and through the busy traffic. His touch, the feel of his hand on my arm, even through the fabric of my jacket and blouse, had an intensity that burned right through me. I could barely remember when any man had affected me so strongly. And maybe that was it. I felt Stewarton's manly strength. The expensive suit, pristine shirt and tie, belied the core strength of the man himself.

Stewarton had said something to me as we arrived outside the chocolatier's shop and tearoom. The lights shone on to the pavement and we were lit–up together for a moment while he stopped and repeated what he'd said. I hadn't heard him properly because I'd been thinking...well...about how manly he was...and thoughts I hardly dared to acknowledge.

His pale eyes with their dark lashes peered down at me, urging me to listen.

I blinked out of my thoughts and concentrated on the moment. What was so important to him?

'I apologise, Tilsie.'

His words drifted in the air...then I got his meaning. *Santa*. He realised I'd been telling the truth when I'd blamed Santa for the windy outburst in the knitting shop months ago.

I nodded. Apology accepted, though I didn't really want to discuss it further. One round of embarrassment was enough.

He opened the door for me and I stepped inside the shop.

The vintage tearoom was a chocolate–lover's dream. The tearoom was part of the shop and the aroma of chocolate, vanilla and baking drifted tastefully through the premises.

86

Sweet stands were artfully piled with confectionary, many wrapped in gold and silver paper. Boxes of handmade chocolates were displayed on the shelves, and the cakes ranged from white chocolate miniatures to lavish milk chocolate cakes and tiered dark chocolate masterpieces. Everything about the chocolatier's shop had a luxurious quality and even though Christmas was several weeks away, shiny baubles hung in the window and fairy lights gave a hint that the festive season was drawing near. A few Christmas trees and decorations had already popped up in the city shops and Edinburgh had a sense of anticipation of the busy Christmas season.

We sat opposite each other at a table for two, giving me plenty of time to study him. My goodness he was a handsome man.

But handsome men could be trouble. And I had no intention of repeating my past mistakes. Just because he was gorgeous, single, pleased to see me and tempting me with luscious chocolate confections didn't mean anything.

'Caelan's a friend of mine,' said Stewarton as we studied the menu. 'He's not in this evening but I can recommend the white and dark chocolate truffles.'

'Agnes recommended the chocolate fudge cake.' I searched for it on the menu.

Stewarton pointed to the cakes on display, works of art almost too wonderful to eat. 'That's the fudge cake over there. Agnes' recommendation is one that I might take. It looks delicious.'

I admired the gleaming glass cabinets and elegant wood surroundings. 'The chocolatier has asked Agnes to knit a special tea cosy for his display. She's almost finished it. It's lovely.'

'I'm sure Caelan will appreciate it. He's always been one to acknowledge skilful work.'

'You seem to know him well.'

'Well enough, though I doubt anyone knows him that well. Caelan is a lone wolf sort, though there are those that say the same about me. We used to train together when we were younger.'

'Train? You trained as a chocolatier?'

He laughed. 'No, my culinary skills are dismal. I enjoy my food. I just don't have the skill to cook it.'

'What type of training then?'

'Fight training.'

'You're a fighter?' In that suit? He looked nothing like I imagined a man who could fight would look like. Stewarton was the epitome of high–class business elegance.

He nodded.

'You don't look like a brawler to me.'

'I'm not, though I'm interested to know what you think a brawler would look like.'

'I'm not sure but...maybe it's the posh suit and the air of snooty nose about you that makes it hard to believe you could handle yourself in a fight.' I held up my fists and pretended to jab at him.

And of course that's when the waiter, looking every bit as elegant as the tearoom surroundings, arrived to take our order. The look he gave me. It was almost as bad as the one Stewarton had given me when he'd blamed me for the disgusting noise that Santa had made. I put my fists down nonchalantly and tried not to give a rat's.

'She's had a hectic day,' Stewarton said, smirking at the waiter.

'Haven't we all,' the waiter replied. 'Can I suggest tonight's speciality — a pot of hot chocolate laced with essences created by our master chocolatier?'

Oh yes. I was up for some of that. And a slice of the chocolate fudge cake and the truffles. The hectic day, the hectic week in fact, warranted a lavish indulgence.

I gazed over at Stewarton as he spoke to the waiter, admiring that handsome face of his and those gorgeous grey eyes that could look so cool and yet flickered with mischief whenever he looked at me.

My stomach knotted and I felt a blush break across my cheeks just thinking about him, wondering what it would be like to kiss those firm lips and run my hands through his silky dark hair. The brooding looks that had first caught my attention were urging me to succumb to all lavish indulgences on offer that night.

But then a warning kicked in. Men like Stewarton didn't love women like me. They loved the Julie types of this world, and apart from the superficial similarities, I was nothing like her.

88

Chapter Ten

Chocolate Cake

The chocolate fudge cake tasted delicious and the truffles were melt in the mouth perfection. Stewarton's cake was covered in rich, shiny ganache and cream. He let me taste a bite and even shared his salt caramels and champagne truffles with me.

We chatted about the conference and he ordered another pot of chocolate and a pot of tea. Sheer indulgence.

'This is a list of all the businesses attending.' He handed me the list. I skimmed the names of companies and individuals. I recognised a few because I'd done business with them during my corporate work or current marketing. I noticed two names in particular. Most of the names were listed by category. There were two chocolatiers who were attending. One of them was a guest speaker and it wasn't Caelan Broadie.

'I see there's another chocolatier who is a guest speaker.'

'Jaec Midwinter. Yes, he's moved premises. He used to have a shop on the West Coast but now he's in one of the vintage shops in Feingold's shopping complex chateau.'

'I've met him. When I worked for the marketing company I was scheduled to deal with his account but he decided to do his own marketing.'

'I try to have a diverse range of speakers from various types of businesses. Even though there are few chocolatiers, there will be those who are interested in hearing how a mid–range business handles its marketing. I asked Caelan, but it's not his sort of thing. He was the one who suggested Midwinter.'

'No rivalry there then?'

'None that I've seen. Few of us have time for rivalry these days. We're all too busy trying to get on with our own business.'

He brought tickets for the event from his jacket pocket. The expensive lining of his jacket shone like liquid pewter and was a fair match for the tie he was wearing. Both were several shades darker than those pale grey eyes of his that seemed to see right through me and yet continued to gaze at me as if I was the most interesting person he knew. Both looks unnerved me, and excited me. There was something about Stewarton that evoked extremes of emotions and I knew I'd find it difficult to concentrate entirely on business when this gorgeous man was sitting opposite me and smiling straight at me.

'As a speaker at the event, you're entitled to three VIP tickets to invite guests to attend all aspects of the conference.' He put the tickets down on the table in front of me. The event cost a small fortune and I immediately knew the first person I wanted to invite.

I picked up the tickets which were embossed with silver lettering. Very posh. Very Stewarton. 'I'd like to invite Agnes if that's okay with you.'

'Indeed.'

'And Agnes' friend, Lisa. She owns a gift shop.'

'Two business women and friends. I'm sure they'll enjoy the event. It starts on Friday and there's a soirée in the evening. Dinner and dancing basically, so they'll need their party frocks.'

'I can imagine how excited they'll be. The knitting bee is going to be buzzing.'

'And what about you? Will you be up for a dance? Or will it be strictly business?'

'Mainly business. Maybe not strictly business. I want to give a talk that will be useful in marketing terms, and hopefully interesting. When I had to give presentations, keeping the audience's interest was a priority, and offering advice that's of use. I thought I'd concentrate on talking about various aspects of the marketing mix and how each one affects small to medium size businesses. Although I work mostly with craft businesses, I have experience across the board. I don't pretend to be an expert but hopefully I can talk about things people will recognise, things that matter at the core of most business ventures. And I'll let the high flyers talk the game up from there.'

He was nodding as I spoke. 'I like the sound of that. Quite a few of the speakers will be talking the high game so if you could cover the smaller business aspects of marketing, particularly cost–effective methods for advertising and promotions, that would be ideal.'

'I'll prepare notes and be ready for the conference. How many talks will I have to give? And do they have to vary?'

'Three talks. One on the Friday around mid–day. One on Saturday afternoon. It would be great if you could vary those. Then one on the Sunday morning. The conference finishes with a céilidh on the Sunday evening. The Saturday evening festive ball is glamorous but more subdued. On Sunday night everyone lets their hair down.' He gave me a copy of the detailed schedule.

'You said it's being held in a country house estate?'

'Yes, they hire their grand hall out for conferences of this type and the kitchens deal with all the catering. Rooms, although limited, are available for guests, but I make arrangements for hotels in the city to provide accommodation if needed. Most of the businesses live within the area. Those travelling from further away tend to make their own arrangements or have already booked a room at the estate.'

'You must be very busy getting everything ready.'

'It took quite a bit of organising the first year, then each year as everyone continued to want to be involved, things became less hectic. This is the fourth year now.'

I lifted up my cup of hot chocolate that had been freshly poured and sprinkled with chocolate flakes. 'Here's to a successful conference, Stewarton.'

'And to many more to come.'

We clinked our cups of hot chocolate and drank a sweet toast to the event ahead.

The third ticket lay unaccounted for on the table.

'As I'm inviting two ladies, I thought I'd ask a man to join us. I hope that would be okay?'

He nodded tentatively. Perhaps he noted the hesitation in my voice. I wondered whether or not to invite this man, but it seemed like the right thing to do.

'I haven't spoken to him for a while, but I'd like to make the offer of the ticket to him. He may not want to go, but I think he would enjoy himself, and we all know each other and he's in business that could benefit from the conference.'

The pale grey eyes darkened almost to the tone of his silk tie. Any smile he'd had faded.

'Is everything okay?' I asked.

'I wondered if you'd want to ask him if I gave you the tickets. I almost didn't want to offer them to you, then I thought how silly I was. Ewan's back I hear.'

'Ewan's back?' That was news to me.

'Back this morning. Not that I've been keeping a careful eye on him. I'm not in the least bit concerned that he'd try to sweet talk you into dating him again.'

I almost spluttered into my chocolate. 'Sweet talk?'

He shrugged and looked uncomfortable. 'You know what I mean. I was trying to put it politely.'

I shook my head at him. 'It wasn't Ewan I wanted to invite.'

The grey eyes flashed across at me. 'No?'

'No. It was Matt. He owns the mountaineering shop. He's a bit of a handful. Full of mischief, but he's a kind sort at heart and I reckon that Agnes and Lisa can keep him in line.'

'Matt?' The relief on Stewarton's face lifted his features again.

'Yes. Though he may insist on wearing his kilt and he's very traditional when he wears it.' I gave him a knowing look.

'Ah. He goes commando.'

I pressed my lips together and nodded.

'So do the majority who wear their kilts to the céilidh, though I'm not saying whether or not I'm the traditional sort.'

'You'll be wearing a kilt?'

'Only on the Sunday night for the céilidh. Friday and Saturday it's a suit as usual. Far more me. Though I do wear a gold pin in my kilt,' he joked. 'I have to keep up the snobby aspect after all.'

'Will I have to wear a dress suitable for the occasion?'

'Most of the ladies wear evening dresses on Friday night, ball gowns on Saturday evening, and full–length dresses on Sunday too, some tartan or suitable for a céilidh. The main things are shoes. Wear your dancing shoes, Tilsie.'

'I've only ever been to one céilidh at a New Year party a few years ago. I danced my socks off and I'm not even a dancer.'

'Expect a repeat of that with bells on. The céilidh is the highlight of the parties.'

I now felt as excited as I anticipated Agnes and Lisa would be.

Having discussed further aspects of the convention, the conversation veered back round to Ewan.

'I expect he'll be in touch with you. Tomorrow perhaps,' said Stewarton.

I shrugged my shoulders. 'I'm not interested in hearing from him. He's left things a bit late to mend any bridges with me.'

'Some men have a way with them to persuade a woman to forgive them their faults.'

I toyed with the last chocolate–coated salt caramel on my plate. 'It won't make any difference. I'm not interested in romance for the foreseeable future. I don't have time to deal with my business, especially at this time of year, and become inveigled in the drama of romance.'

'It sounds as if you've made up your mind.'

'I have,' I said firmly, and popped the last sweet in my mouth.

The cold night air swept along the street as we walked back up to the knitting shop where both our cars were parked.

The lights were on in the shop and I could see Agnes knitting behind the counter. She didn't notice us at first and then she waved out.

'I suppose my ears will be burning within the next ten minutes.'

I shook my head. 'Five.'

He nodded in agreement.

'Well,' he said. 'I guess I'll see you at the conference. I'll email any details as things get closer to the conference dates, and contact me if you need to know anything or change your mind about being one of the speakers.'

'Why would I change my mind?'

He gave a half–hearted shrug, and suddenly I saw the young man in him, the one who had trained to fight alongside Caelan the chocolatier. Two young men with a grudge against the world, determined to punch well above their weight when it came to building their careers, though that was not to be in the boxing ring or martial arts world, and it had left them both with a skill that would last a lifetime.

He sighed, and I heard the weary tone in his voice even though he tried to hide it. 'When it comes to romance, I'm always out of step. It's always too early or too late to get involved with someone I'm interested in. My timing is always wrong. And sadly, it's wrong again — with you, Tilsie.'

I didn't need him to wring out every detail. I knew if I hadn't insisted that I'd put romance on hold in favour of business, Stewarton would've asked me out on another dinner date and we'd have taken things from there. Instead, we were once again heading off in separate directions, planning to meet only for business at the conference. Bad timing for Stewarton again. And maybe for me. Was I making a mistake letting Stewarton drive out of my life again? Maybe, but I let him go, watching the tail lights of his car disappear along the street.

I wrapped my arms around myself and shivered in the cold night air, though the wintry night wasn't entirely responsible for the coldness I felt. But I couldn't risk everything again on yet another broken heart, certainly not now when I had so many businesses wanting me to help them with their marketing. It was difficult, and yet easier to let the hope of love drift in favour of the safe option of making my business work, building my independence, and finding solace and cheer in the company of Agnes and the knitting bee ladies. They never let me down. Men, on the other hand, always had.

I turned and walked into the shop.

Five minutes later I was sitting with a cup of tea and telling Agnes what happened. I reckoned Stewarton's ears were on fire.

Chapter Eleven

Romance & Knitting

'I knew it,' said Agnes, sounding delighted. 'I knew Stewarton had a twinkle in his eyes for you.'

I explained about putting romance on the back burner.

She continued to knit what looked like a large tinsel bauble while I relayed all the details of what had happened. I hadn't even told her about the party invitations. One thing at a time, I thought. She was hyper enough discussing my love life, or lack of it, and whether I'd made the right decision about giving Stewarton the flick.

'I wouldn't exactly say I'd given him the flick,' I said, wondering if this was true.

Agnes frowned over the top of her spectacles at me.

'Okay, so I sort of gave him the flick.'

'Maybe he'll fight for you. Maybe he won't take no for an answer.'

'Stewarton trained as a fighter,' I said.

She stopped knitting.

'He told me he trained with the chocolatier, Caelan Broadie, years ago.'

She started knitting again. 'Caelan can certainly handle himself in a fight. He's even got fighter tattoos — on his arms, not anywhere else, or so I've heard.'

'Apparently, they've been friends for years, but he says that Caelan doesn't want to give a talk at the conference, so he's asked another chocolatier, Jaec Midwinter, to be one of the speakers.'

'Oh it sounds so glamorous. A soirée on the Friday, glam ball and then a céilidh. You'll have to take loads of pictures to show me and the girls.'

I looked at her.

She paused from knitting the... 'What is that you're knitting, Agnes?'

She held it up. 'A gold tea cosy. I thought I'd make something special for Caelan's chocolatier shop just in case he doesn't like the chocolate tea cosy. This yarn looks like sparkle but it knits up great.' She pulled it to show how stretchy it was.

I had no need for another tea cosy. I had one teapot at home and several cosies. I loved to knit them. I'd succumbed to making a bumblebee tea cosy during the summer and even made the little bumble softie to go with it. Agnes had some great patterns for cosies including a butterfly one that was very popular with customers.

During the past few months I'd become even more passionate about my knitting. I found it soothing, giving my hands something to do, helping me unwind after a trying day.

'Is there something I can knit?' I said, my fingers itching to tackle a few rows while I wondered how to tell her about Ewan being back and about the VIP tickets.

I hardly needed to ask. 'Help yourself,' she said, opening a cupboard door beside the counter. 'I've lots of patterns that need knitting up for the Christmas displays. If you could knit up two wee Christmas trees to finish off the festive bunting that would be appreciated. And I've jumpers that need knitted.' She thrust one jumper at me. 'This one has Christmas balls on the front, knitted into the pattern. Could you finish it for me? Lisa is tackling the reindeer jumper. She's always had a knack for knitting realistic antlers.'

I made a start on the Christmas trees, knitting garter stitch trees with sparkly green, red and gold yarn.

'So,' she said, as we settled down to knit together while having our tea, 'you were telling me about the festive ball at the conference. Have you thought what type of dress you'll wear?'

Here goes I thought. 'I thought we should maybe try to coordinate our dresses.' I continued knitting.

'What do you mean?'

'Stewarton gave me three VIP tickets to all the events at the conference. I get to invite three guests. I thought you'd like to go. And Lisa.'

I thought she was going to hug me to pieces.

After she let me go, she said, 'What about the third ticket?'

'I thought I'd invite Matt.'

She laughed and seemed to approve of my choice. 'He'll insist on wearing his kilt.'

'I warned Stewarton. I remembered you telling me about Matt and his kilt.'

'He'll be a good laugh to have along with us. I can't wait to tell Lisa. Dresses. We'll all need dresses. Except Matt of course, though that kilt of his is due an airing.'

We chatted, plotted and planned for the next hour and then jumped when a man knocked on the window of the shop. Whoever it was had boxes, gift wrapped, piled up in his arms, so high I had to look carefully to see who he was.

'It's Ewan,' Agnes hissed.

'I forgot to mention,' I said. 'Stewarton told me Ewan arrived back this morning.'

'How does Stewarton know and we don't? He must be keeping a watchful eye on the competition.'

'What competition?'

She pursed her lips at me. 'If Stewarton wants to date you then he's savvy enough to know that his main rival is Ewan.'

Ewan knocked insistently on the window.

'I'd better open the door,' said Agnes. 'Hide behind the Christmas display if you don't want to talk to him.'

I decided to face him. I'd need to talk to him some time.

Agnes' welcome gave a clear indication of how happy we were to see him back.

'What do you want at this time of night?' Agnes snapped at him.

He held the boxes tight. 'I come bearing gifts and a ton of apologies.'

'Gifts, eh?' Agnes shook her head. 'It'll take more than a few trinkets to win us over. Isn't that right, Tilsie?'

I nodded. I couldn't even find it in me to utter one word to him. He looked as handsome as ever, and my heart squeezed seeing him again, but perhaps not in the way it had before. My heart tightened, as if getting ready to defend itself.

'Can I come in? It's spitting rain. I don't want the parcels to get soaked.'

She stepped aside and he came in and put the parcels down on the counter. He eyed the pile of knitting and then turned to face us. 'I understand that you're both upset with me and I've let you down really badly, and for that I am truly sorry.' He looked at Agnes. 'I've heard my absence has caused problems for you at the shop. It was never my intention to do that. I hope in the coming weeks I can make it up to you.'

I felt my resolve weaken. He sounded so sincere. Damn him!

He allowed Agnes to get her wind out, complaining about how she'd had to explain to his customers where he was.

'I'm sorry about that, Agnes. Really, I am. I've no intention of doing anything like that again. In fact, I'm thinking of moving premises, over to the other side of the city centre to a larger shop where I can keep some of my stock. Having it all at the house isn't practical.'

'You're moving away?' she said.

'Thinking about it. But not until next year, in the spring, maybe not at all.' He sounded vague, the way he had before when he'd hinted he might be heading to New York and then he upped and went within a day.

My resolve was still weak. I didn't entirely trust him, but there he was, bending over backwards to apologise and make things up to us. What more could he do, I thought? People made mistakes. I'd made plenty. At least he had the guts to come in and admit he'd mucked up.

Within half an hour he was sitting with us having tea and biscuits and helping Agnes wind a skein of wool into a manageable ball. I got the impression he'd even have attempted to knit a few rows of a jumper if it helped get him back in our good books.

I had tea but no biscuits. I was stuffed with chocolate cake and truffles and buzzing from having eaten too much chocolate. I admitted this to him.

'There's no such thing,' he said, joking with me, as we started to become friendly again. 'Not when it comes to chocolate, especially from the chocolatier.'

Finally, he left.

Agnes locked the door, leaned against it and sighed. 'Did we just forgive that charming bastard?'

'I believe we did.'

She held an end of the bunting I'd finished knitting and we pinned it up as part of the display in the vintage part of the shop. The fairy lights twinkled and rain began to batter off the windows. Inside the shop felt cosy, safe, a haven of knitting and sewing, of crafts and Christmas cheer.

I gazed out at the rainy street and wondered what to do about Ewan. Oh so handsome and charming Ewan. But something in my heart just wouldn't feel the same about him.

'Sleep on it,' Agnes advised.

Agnes had told him about the VIP tickets and he'd said he planned to buy a ticket and attend the conference. He wanted me to promise him a dance.

'Did I agree to dance with Ewan?' I said softly.

'Yes, but you can always use it as an excuse to stamp on his toes with your heels and kick his shins.'

I liked her attitude. I smiled at her.

'Come on,' she said. 'We'll have another cuppa before I lock up.'

I nodded.

'What do you think is in the parcels?' she called to me while filling the kettle. We'd taken little notice of his gifts.

'He said he'd brought us some things from New York and new items he's got in stock. Will we open them now?'

'Yes. I didn't like to accept them when he first arrived and then as we got chatting he never mentioned them again and I didn't like to look keen.'

We opened one each. Mine had novelty salt and pepper pots with a flowery print. 'These would look nice in a vintage–style kitchen.' I handed them to Agnes. 'My kitchen wouldn't suit them.'

'One of the ladies would love these. I'll put them aside for her. She collects things like this for her kitchen.'

Agnes studied the contents of her parcel. 'I like these. Gilded knitting needles. Lovely.'

We decided she should have those.

The other parcels had various selections of dinner napkins for Christmas, festive table runners and cushion covers with appliqué gold Christmas trees. We shared the items and put some aside for Lisa and a couple of the ladies.

I put my jacket on and got ready to leave.

'How did you really feel when you saw Ewan again?' she asked me.

'He's handsome, that's for sure, but I don't feel that I can trust him. Trust is important to me. If I can't trust a man, I could never love him.'

'Maybe he'll win your trust back?'

I got ready to make a run for it in the rain to my car. 'And maybe he won't.'

I drove home in the rain with the wipers at full. I had a lot to think about — and presentations to prepare for the conference. And dresses to buy, borrow or purloin. Whenever I found my thoughts wandering to regrets about Ewan, about forgiving him so easily, I tried to think about the dresses, something nice, something frivolous in a complicated world.

Chapter Twelve

The Vintage Ball Gown

I bought two dresses from Delphine's shop. Both were total bargains. One was a beaded vintage dress that I planned to wear for the Friday party. So classy. A champagne sheath dress sparkling with beads. It was cocktail length and Delphine advised me what shoes and accessories to wear with it so that I looked stylish without appearing as if I'd stepped out of another era.

'Mix vintage with modern to avoid looking like you're wearing fancy dress,' said Delphine.

Good advice.

'There are several beads and diamante missing from the dress,' said Delphine. 'Would you like me to repair those for you?'

'No, I'll sort it.' It seemed like an easy task and something I was happy to do. 'Agnes has plenty of beads and sequins in her haberdashery.'

The second dress was a vintage ball gown. It was hanging on a rail of full–length dresses made from chiffon, silk and organza. She described the colour as sea foam which suited the palest hint of blue/green on the cream fabric. It had layers of chiffon and silk, moved light as air and made me feel like I really was dressed to go to a ball when I wore it.

'It was made for you, Tilsie. The colour suits your pale complexion and the length is right. Though perhaps the waistline needs a couple of darts taken in.'

It looked like a dress that had been loved but rarely worn, maybe only to one ball, two at the most. I loved the idea that the dresses had a story to them, and that my story was about to be added.

And so I bought both dresses. I didn't find anything suitable for the céilidh but I thought I had something in my wardrobe that would suffice. Unfortunately, when I got home and trawled through my wardrobe I realised it wasn't there and that I'd given it away during a clearout.

'We'll make a dress for you,' said Agnes when I told her that I was one dress short for the party events. Agnes and Lisa had already organised their dresses, either wearing something they already had or sewing something special. The ladies at the knitting bee were happy to become involved in our plans, and Wednesday nights spilled into extra evenings when Agnes kept the shop open and we'd all knit and sew.

'I usually keep the shop open late on the run–up to Christmas,' said Agnes. 'We're all busy knitting and sewing gifts and items to decorate the Christmas trees.' She had a selection of patterns to make sparkly baubles from wool and felt and I wished I had time to make some. But I had enough to do with work, planning my talks and getting my outfits ready. And then there was the dancing. My heart sank when I thought about it.

'Have a look at my new fabrics,' said Agnes, leading me over to the Christmas range and pulling out a bolt of cotton silk printed with tiny Christmas trees. The print reminded me of a plaid, especially with the festive colours, and viewed from a distance it had a tartan–like quality to it and yet it was comprised of little Christmas trees.

'I love it,' I said, falling for it at once.

She went to show me other fabrics but I'd already set my heart on the Christmas tree print. Now all we had to do was find a pattern, but of course, Agnes' range of dress patterns came up with a simple and yet very attractive design.

'We'll help run this up for you, Tilsie,' said Agnes. 'I've been wondering what this fabric would look like when sewn into a dress. Maybe after the party you'll let me borrow it to put it on my new mannequin in my window display.'

'New mannequin?' I'd hurried into the shop, sheltering under my umbrella, and hadn't noticed.

'I liked Hetty and saw this one on sale so I snapped her up,' Agnes said proudly. 'She's a wire vintage model similar to Hetty.'

'She's perfect,' I said. 'And yes, you can have the dress to display after the party.'

'Great. Let's make a start on the cutting.'

By the time the week of the conference arrived in late November, the shops were ablaze with Christmas lights and festive decorations. The weather had taken another step forward into the depths of winter and snow covered the streets — a light sprinkling, but snow that wasn't prepared to melt. More snow was forecast so we knew we were in for a cold snap.

'My kilt's back from the dry cleaners and I've bought three new pairs of socks,' Matt announced as he came into the knitting shop on the Wednesday night and helped himself to a cup of tea and a chocolate Santa biscuit. One of the ladies had baked them and brought a box of them in for everyone to share. She was practising her Christmas dinner menu. The following week she was baking iced mince pies and tipsy fruit sponge cakes and we were all looking forward to sampling those.

The knitting bee was busy with members helping Agnes, Lisa and me with our party outfits, and getting on with their Christmas knitting. There were blankets being crocheted, jumpers and hats knitted and quilts sewn.

The ladies who were handy with a sewing needle stitched diamante on to our dresses. Everyone in the knitting bee was sharing in the excitement of the three–party event, for that's what it had become. Agnes and Lisa intended to circulate and make business contacts, and to cheer me on during my talks, but the highlights of the conference event were the parties in the evenings.

'Is Fay giving you a hard time because you'll be out three nights gadding about with us?' Lisa asked Matt.

'No,' he said, parking his deflated backside on the edge of the shop counter. 'She's been a real sweetheart about it. She wanted me to go to a weekend music concert with her before Tilsie invited me to the parties, and it wasn't really my sort of thing. So she's going out with the girls and having a rare time with them while I party with you, Agnes and Tilsie.'

'That's worked out nicely then,' said Lisa.

Matt nodded. 'Fay says she trusts me. She's a wee smasher. She really boosts my confidence. She said to me last night that how she looks on things is like this — before she met me there were few women who wanted up my kilt so there's precious little chance of them wanting me nowadays. Not many men have girlfriends who say lovely things like that. She says that's why we get on so well because she thinks I'm the bee's knees.' He beamed with delight while we eyed each other, not wishing to disillusion him.

One of the ladies held up my beaded sheath dress from Delphine's shop. She'd added diamante to the hemline and other parts where the gems had been lost through time and wear. It sparkled under the lights. She smiled at me. 'You'll dazzle them in this dress.'

Then she held up my ball gown. 'And I think Tilsie will look beautiful in this dress.'

I thanked her for helping with the final touches. She'd been a seamstress before she'd retired and had made a lovely job of helping alter the ball gown so that it fitted me like a dream.

'I'm beginning to have second thoughts about my ball gown,' said Lisa. 'I tried it on last night after finishing it. When I saw myself in the mirror all I thought was — you look like a sweetie wrapper. I may have been a smidgen enthusiastic with the shiny ribbon embellishments.'

Agnes disagreed. 'I saw Lisa's dress last night and it's a knockout. Suits her to a tee. We'll all complement each other and dazzle their eyes.'

The seamstress hung my dress up and put it near the window. Agnes's mannequin wore items from the range of Christmas cardigans, jumpers and accessories. My dress glittered under the fairy lights that were draped across the window display. A wave of excitement went through me. Only a couple of nights until the Friday event. I was ready with my talks and had practised until I knew what I wanted to say backwards. I was ready. The ladies had helped with the dresses and I had my business suits, tailored skirt suits, all set. But every time I thought about the conference, it wasn't getting up on the stage and giving a talk that made my stomach fill with butterflies. I was lucky. Things like that had never bothered me. And now I wouldn't be walking into the parties on my own. I was going with Matt and the girls, and my dresses were beautiful, so no worries there. I certainly wasn't a dancer, so that concerned me, but Matt had promised to give me a few lessons. No, the thing that gave me butterflies was the thought of seeing Stewarton again. And that made me nervous. Why was I so anxious about seeing him? I'd already decided to put romance on the back burner.

I hadn't seen Ewan since he'd come loaded with gifts to apologise. Since then, he'd disappeared back into his own busy business life. Agnes had seen him, but as I hadn't returned his emails inviting me to have a dinner date with him, I hadn't heard a peep from him. He was going to the conference, so I'd see him there. And he'd told Agnes he'd been sussing out new premises and definitely planned to move to another shop.

In his last email he'd also said he was looking forward to seeing me at the conference and reminded me I'd promised to dance with him.

Agnes nudged me. 'You've got furrows on that wee brow of yours. What's up?'

'Just thinking about seeing Stewarton and Ewan again,' I said quietly while the knitting bee buzzed cheerfully around us.

'Don't you fret about them. You'll soon know if either of them is the man for you when you dance with them.'

'Dance with them?' My voice pitched so high it rose above the clickety–clack of numerous sets of knitting needles and chatter.

'Of course you're going to dance with them. That's one of the ways I used to tell if a man was for me. You can tell from the way he holds you. It's just different from talking to a man, obviously, or even canoodling. Dancing together...well...you either feel right or your don't. And it's got nothing to do with whether they can dance or not. Most people aren't great dancers but it doesn't stop us waltzing around a dance floor. It's the man you're with that matters, and how you feel when you're in his arms, when you're close to him. And how he feels about you. There are few things more romantic, because he has to restrain taking things further when all eyes are watching you on the dance floor. That's why I used to go by that when I was younger. I still do, though chances to go to posh dances like these are few and far between these days.'

'Maybe you'll get yourself a man at one of the parties,' Matt said to her, overhearing our conversation.

She smiled. 'You never know, Matt. You haven't seen the dress I've knitted for the Saturday night. It hugs my body and gives me curves where I need them and flattens the ones I don't want.'

Matt's eyes widened. 'You've knitted an evening dress? You're wearing a woolly ball gown?'

'Calm down. It doesn't look like a giant tea cosy if that's what you're thinking,' she told him. 'It's elegance personified. Isn't it girls?'

Every head around him nodded.

'Agnes is going to surprise everyone with her dress,' said Lisa. She winked at us and then added, 'There's still time to knit you a kilt, Matt. You'd look a treat and stand out from all the other kilties.'

It was time for Matt to leave. 'Thanks for the offer, ladies, but I'll stick to my tartan.'

'Speaking of sticking to your tartan,' Agnes reminded him. 'You'd better be wearing breeks under that burly kilt of yours.'

'See you later,' he said and hurried out.

Agnes shook her head at us. 'He's going to be ball naked.'

We laughed and continued with our knitting and sewing and gossiping about all the things we planned to do at the parties.

Later that night I lay in bed thinking about Ewan. I remembered what Delphine had asked me. 'What if Ewan comes back and realises he made a mistake and has missed you all these weeks he's been away? You seemed to really like him that evening you went out to dinner.'

I had liked him, and people did make mistakes. Was ignoring the dinner date emails from Ewan a mistake? Or was the biggest mistake the bad timing with Stewarton? I was too tired to work out the answers, and fell asleep thinking about the conference and gazing at the first flakes of snow on the window...

Chapter Thirteen

Winter Snow

The city was covered in snow. My plans to wear shoes to the first day of the conference were scuppered. I needed boots and a warmer coat. Even though I was driving there, the roads were white with snow and I reckoned by the time I arrived at the estate I may have to walk from the main car park to reach the house.

I navigated through the icy terrain and parked as near to the house as possible. What I assumed were the front lawns were covered in snow and attendants were out to direct people to where they needed to go. The car park was already busy.

Stewarton had emailed to confirm the final details, though his messages had been businesslike. Polite and yet distant. It hardly seemed real that we'd enjoyed an evening together at the chocolatier's shop not so long ago. But it was me who had insisted I wasn't interested in romance, so I couldn't blame Stewarton for doing as I'd asked.

I had my laptop and briefcase with me as I trudged through the snow. I'd also brought a pair of shoes to change into, so I was loaded down when I arrived at the front entrance. The doors were open and I could feel the warmth welcome me in. I hoped to receive the same welcome from Stewarton. My stomach had been knotted all morning, and I'd been so worked up about everything I hadn't been able to eat breakfast. My tummy rumbled in the car and I hoped I could get something to eat before giving my talk which was scheduled for mid–day. Two of us were speaking during the hour before lunch. I was the second speaker and had been allocated half an hour. I'd rehearsed what I'd talk about which included things I'd spoken about before many times at the company presentations which often fell to me to handle.

The house was the equivalent of a large mansion converted for business conferences and party events. I think it also catered for weddings. Ewan would love that.

I showed my pass to one of the attendants and was escorted through to the main hall, shown the stage and then led to where I could leave my things while mingling with others until it was time to give my talk. I sat down on a bench and took my boots off. They were thick with snow. I'd worn a pair of socks over my tights and was taking them off to put my shoes on when I heard a familiar voice.

'I'm glad you got here safely, Tilsie.'

I looked up and there was Stewarton, immaculate as always in a dark suit that was as classy as the man wearing it.

His hair was swept back from his handsome features and I found myself hit with a wave of emotion when I saw him. It was like looking at a man I used to know, someone I'd been close to, who was now part of my past and never to be my future. I was so overwhelmed I could've burst into tears. I'd never ever felt like that before.

'Are you okay?' He came over and his closeness made the effect he had on me all the more potent.

'Eh...yes...' My tummy rumbled and I used it as an excuse for my reaction. 'I skipped breakfast. I think I need a cup of tea and something to eat.'

Taking me at my word, he called to someone to organise tea and a light snack for me.

I stood there in my stocking soles with him towering above me. Even when I stepped into my black court shoes I still only came up to his shoulders. Such broad shoulders. Such a damn handsome man.

Calm down, I told myself firmly. Maybe I did just need some tea and toast. It couldn't be that I had feelings this strong for Stewarton. Could I?

I felt his eyes study me, wondering what the hell was wrong with me.

I turned away from his gaze and hung my coat up then tucked my boots under the bench.

When I turned back he was still watching me with a look of...I wasn't sure what the look was in his eyes. Those gorgeous pale grey eyes of his had always been unreadable.

He smiled gently. 'It's good to see you again, Tilsie.'

I smiled nervously and tried to keep my voice steady. 'It's good to see you again too.'

And it was. It really was. I wanted to give him a hug and tell him how pleased I was to see him. But I didn't. I kept my promise to myself not to make any silly mistakes again when it came to romance. Today, this weekend, I had to concentrate on working hard to give my talks, my presentations, and earn the substantial amount of money he was paying me as a guest speaker. There was no room for nonsense, though I supposed when Matt and the girls arrived for the party at night, there would be plenty of that, unintentional or not.

'Is Agnes and her friend coming as guests? And Matt?'

'Yes. They were delighted with the invitations, thank you. Agnes wanted to be here for my talk but I thought the party tonight would be sufficient. They'll all be here this evening, and then again for the full day on Saturday.'

'And the ball? Will they be there? Will you?'

'Yes. Dresses at the ready. I bought a ball gown.' I could hear myself start to babble but Stewarton seemed interested in everything I said. 'Sorry, I definitely need that tea, I'm chattering on and on.'

'No, I'm glad to chat to you and hear all about your dress. I'm sure it'll be spectacular.'

'And we're all going to the céilidh. Matt's wearing his kilt, but Agnes has warned him that he can't go commando.'

'Sounds like it'll be quite an interesting weekend.'

There was a pause as he lingered close to me. Did he want to kiss me? The way he studied my face, my mouth, I felt as if he did.

'Excuse me, Stewarton,' a man said from the doorway. 'The press have arrived and we're trying to organise the photos. Some of the guests are held up due to the snow and haven't arrived yet so we're asking if anyone else would care to step in for the press photos.'

'Would you like to join us?' Stewarton said to me. 'I'd actually taken the liberty of putting your name down for the press call as you're one of the speakers.'

'Eh...yes. That's fine.' I wondered if my hair looked a mess. I'd worn it up in a chignon but the wind had blown wildly as I'd got into the car to drive here and I hadn't bothered to check to see if it was okay. My suit comprised of a black skirt, cut just below the knee, worn with a white blouse and a fitting black jacket with a small velvet collar.

The man led the way to the main hall where the press were waiting. Stewarton walked beside me. He whispered to me as we stepped into the vast hall where the stage was lit up. 'You look great. Really great.'

I took the compliment the way he'd intended it. At least, I thought I did. He could obviously see that I was somewhat anxious about being thrown into the press shots unprepared.

I was introduced to a couple of the journalists who noted my name and what I did. Then about ten of us lined up to have our photographs taken. Two other speakers were in the line up, along with Stewarton and other business people. Stewarton managed to manoeuvre me so we were standing together in the photos.

Afterwards, I was led into one of the mansion's elegant dining rooms where I was served tea and sandwiches. The table was set with white linen and the whole room was beautifully elegant. I gazed out the bay windows at the snow. The trees surrounding the mansion were iced white and vast areas of the ground were untouched. Not a footstep. Just pure white snow. I breathed, taking it all in, feeling better with a cup of tea and something to eat.

'There you are,' a man said. 'I was looking for you.'

I glanced towards the doorway and there was Ewan.

'Stewarton said you hadn't had breakfast and they were feeding you before you give your presentation. I didn't want to miss it. How are you? You're looking lovely as ever.'

His words were smooth, pouring from his sensual lips, and I felt myself watch him and listen, as if detached. His handsomeness did affect me. I couldn't deny it. But more than anything, I wished he hadn't turned up at the conference and that I didn't have to wonder how I felt about him.

How did I feel about him? Seeing him again? The same as before, I decided. Nothing had changed. I still didn't trust him even though I wanted to.

He came over and sat down at the table. He relaxed back in his chair and commented on the view. 'It's like a winter wonderland out there. I hear we're in for a harsh winter, though if the snow keeps up, we could have a white Christmas. Less than four weeks now until Christmas. Any plans for the holidays?'

'No, no plans. Hopefully I'll be at home with my feet up watching old films and eating too much festive food.'

'On your own?'

'Yes.'

'So I've got time to persuade you otherwise.'

Before I could reply that I wasn't interested in spending Christmas with him, Stewarton came to my rescue.

'When you've finished your tea, could you come along to the stage area to meet the other speakers? Someone hasn't turned up yet. They're stuck in traffic, so we're having to rearrange the schedule.'

I couldn't get up quick enough. 'I'll come with you now.' I gulped down the rest of my tea, grabbed my bag and hurried out.

Ewan kept in step with us. 'I'm eager to hear your talk today,' he said to me. 'And remember you've promised me a dance later. I'm going to hold you to that.'

I smiled tightly.

Stewarton threw Ewan a look that seared right through him. Ewan didn't react. He smiled at me and walked to where most of the guests were mingling and chatting business.

'I didn't mean to interrupt anything,' said Stewarton.

'You didn't.'

'Stewarton,' a man said, 'Jaec Midwinter says he's happy to give his talk to open the proceedings.'

'Excellent,' said Stewarton. 'We'll keep Tilsie as scheduled.'

That meant I was on after Midwinter the chocolatier. I'd no idea what his talk would be, but he had a specialised business so the things I wanted to mention would fit quite well with his.

During the next hour I was introduced to lots of people. Business cards were exchanged and contacts made. The networking at this event alone was worthwhile.

Finally the audience was seated and the stage was set for the first speaker. Jaec Midwinter's talk was informative and gave a fascinating insight into the marketing he used for his chocolatier's business.

Then it was my turn to take to the stage. The half hour went by quickly, and I think I managed to mention everything I'd intended — from how small niche businesses could benefit from marketing to how the current market had adapted to the latest trends in the marketing mix, particularly advertising and promotions.

No one got up to leave while I was talking so I counted that as a good sign. The applause when I'd finished made me hopeful I'd given the audience information they could think about for their businesses.

Stewarton approached me as I came off stage. 'Well done. That was first–class.'

'I thought the chocolatier was a hard act to follow. He had some really relevant things to talk about.'

'He did, but so did you. I think you both complemented each other.'

Others congratulated me on my talk during the remainder of the day, and as I looked outside the vast window of the conference room, the snow hadn't melted. It looked freezing outside. It was already dark and car headlamps lit up the trees as people came and went.

My dress for the party was in the boot of my car along with the silver and white wrap I'd knitted. If ever there was an evening to wear it, this was surely it. Now all I had to do was put my boots on, trek to the car, collect my dress and then trek back and get changed.

I was putting my boots on when Stewarton offered to help me. 'Give me your car keys and I'll bring your things in. It's freezing outside.'

I gave him my keys and waited in the warmth of the doorway while he trudged through the snow to my car. He had the sense to throw a winter jacket on over his suit and a pair of snow boots.

'Here you are,' he said, smiling at me.

His jacket was zipped up to the neck with a high collar, and for a moment I saw another look to him. With his suit hidden by his ski jacket, he looked even more handsome. Damn these men. They made looking attractive seem so casual. I hoped my vintage beaded dress and knitted wrap would work their magic on me. I planned to keep my hair up in the chignon and wear the fashion necklace that Delphine had suggested along with the only pair of shoes I had that went with the champagne–coloured dress. Shoes with heels I could dance in.

I got dressed and ventured out into the party. The stage had been cleared, and the seating replaced with a dance floor surrounded by dining tables. Dinner was a slightly more casual affair than what was planned for the Saturday festive ball, but it was still grand by ordinary standards.

I felt the excitement build up inside me and went over to admire the large Christmas tree near the patio windows. That's when I saw three figures wave at me from across the room. I waved back, delighted that Agnes, Lisa and Matt had arrived. They all looked great. Matt had one of them on each arm. Matt had worn a dark suit, shirt and tie. He'd told us he was keeping his kilt for the Sunday céilidh. Agnes' dress was dark blue with a layer of chiffon sparkle, while Lisa wore a long black velvet skirt and a glittery top.

I hurried over to greet them.

'How did your talk go?' Agnes said to me before I could tell them how lovely they looked. 'Lisa and I were watching the clock in the shop and wondering how you were getting on. Weren't we?'

'Yes,' said Lisa. 'We were hoping you'd do well.'

'Everything went fine,' I said. 'The audience clapped and the response from people has been great, so I'm pleased that all the notes I made were worthwhile.'

'We knew you'd be smashing,' said Agnes, smiling proudly at me.

'Did you get here okay?' I said. 'I was concerned about the traffic with all this snow.'

'Matt drove us here in his all–terrain car,' said Agnes.

'It can cope with mountain roads and handled the snow without any problems,' Matt said cheerily.

'He lifted us in here so we didn't have to put our boots back on in the car when we arrived,' said Lisa. Then she squirmed. 'I don't like being lifted. I always think I'm too heavy.'

'Nonsense,' said Matt. 'The pair of you are as light as a wee chooky hen's feathers.'

Agnes and Lisa giggled and I could see they were pleased to be with Matt.

An announcement was made that dinner was being served in the main hall and in the restaurant. Couples were also encouraged to step on to the dance floor and we had to restrain Matt from pulling the three of us on for a dance before we'd had a chance to be seated at our table.

'We'll dance later, Matt,' said Agnes. 'Let's get something to eat first.'

'Okay–dokey,' he said, happy to offer us his arms and escort us to our table for four.

Dinner was delicious. A traditional menu with roasts, salmon and fine wines went down a treat.

Matt didn't drink and preferred soft drinks. I tried the mulled ginger wine but as we were all mostly tea lovers, cups of tea kept us fuelled throughout the evening.

The lighting was dimmed slightly after the meals were finished and the whole room had a fairytale atmosphere. The decorations were traditional — gold, red and green and twinkling lights and lanterns lit the room.

'This is lovely I have to say,' said Agnes.

'Are we allowed to take photographs?' Lisa had her phone ready to take some snaps. 'We promised the knitting bee members we'd sent them pictures of what the event looked like and our dresses.'

'Yes,' I said.

Lisa snapped several shots of us and then sent them to one of her knitting friends. 'I've got two of the ladies on standby. I send the photos to them and they send them to all the other members.'

With the knitting bee members now part of the party event, we took to the dance floor with Matt, each taking a turn to waltz with him. Matt was light on his feet for a well–muscled man, and Agnes and Lisa were both adept at social dancing. I was the one who wasn't a very good dancer but I managed to waltz with Matt. 'I'll keep you right,' he said to me. 'Hang on to me and we'll glide around the floor.'

And we did. There were moments when I fluffed up my steps but Matt simply lifted me off the floor without anyone noticing my clumsy steps and we continued from there.

I sat back down at our table with Agnes while Lisa took her turn with Matt.

'He's a biddable soul, isn't he?' Agnes said, looking over at Matt who was making sure Lisa's long skirt didn't get fankled.

'He is. Fay's a lucky lady.'

'I haven't seen Stewarton since he nodded over to us at dinner. How did things go when you met him again?'

I gave her all the details, including what happened with Ewan.

She craned to see over the tables. 'Where is Ewan? Or does he think he's charmed us enough this month?'

'Over there near the Christmas tree chatting to a few people.'

'Do you think he'll make a play for you later tonight?'

'I hope not.'

'Still not entirely trust him?'

114

'No.'

'What about Stewarton?'

I hesitated.

'Ah, so that's the problem.'

'I didn't say a thing.'

'And that says it all.'

'I'm not getting involved with Stewarton,' I said, unaware he was approaching our table and that I'd spoken loud enough for him to hear me.

I cringed when I saw him.

'I didn't think for a moment that you would,' he said softly, as if I'd cut him to the bone.

'I'm sorry, Stewarton, I didn't mean —'

'There's not need to apologise, Tilsie,' he said. 'I'm quite clear regarding things between us, and I'm fine with that, so relax and enjoy the party.'

He walked away and spoke to other guests.

I did enjoy the party. I had a great night with Matt and the girls. We laughed and danced and thoroughly enjoyed ourselves.

Before I realised, it was time to head home.

'Same again tomorrow night, ladies?' said Matt.

We all agreed to meet up for another evening together. This time it was the festive ball.

'We're going to come along in the afternoon to hear your talk,' said Agnes.

Matt nodded. 'Then we'll get changed for the party.'

Agreeing on our plans, I waved them off. Matt insisted on lifting them back across the thick snow, carrying Lisa first and then Agnes.

I waved to them from the doorway and as I turned around there was Ewan. My hands pressed against his firm chest. 'Oh, I didn't see you there, Ewan.'

'I thought you'd be heading home with Agnes.'

'I brought my own car. I'm going to get changed and then drive home.'

'I'd be happy to drive you back, or you could come home with me.'

I blinked and laughed nervously.

He shrugged. 'Can't blame a man for trying.'

'Thanks, but no thanks.'

115

'Another time perhaps when I'm forgiven for everything I did.'

He didn't wait for my reply and walked out into the snow towards his car.

'Is everything all right?'

I glanced round and there was Stewarton.

'Yes. I'm just going to get changed and drive home. I'll be back tomorrow morning around eleven.'

I hurried away, got changed quickly, threw my party things into my bag and headed outside. My boots sank into the deep snow and I hoped my trusty car would start.

I got in and turned the key in the ignition. It started first time. I let the heater and the wipers clear the windscreen and then slowly drove off with only one backwards glance towards the mansion. A figure stood in the doorway, lit up against the backdrop of the Christmas lights. I couldn't see his face clearly but the silhouette was unmistakable. It was Stewarton.

I looked away and concentrated on the road, but my heart had squeezed when I'd seen him watching me leave. Like the first time I'd seen him in the summer, I felt a connection between us.

All the way home I sensed I was in his thoughts. He was certainly in mine, but I was determined to stick to my plan. Romance had brought me nothing but heartache. I needed to take a breather from it and enjoy Christmas without being in love with anyone.

Chapter Fourteen

The Christmas Tree Fabric Dress

A light flurry of snow had fallen overnight. I drove to the conference kitted out for the weather as I had the day before. I wore a grey suit this time. My ball gown was carefully folded in a bag in the boot of the car. I'd also made sure to have breakfast.

The Saturday event was always the busiest and there was certainly a different atmosphere inside the mansion — more intense with business people making deals with each other, and the networking had stepped up a notch. Saturday was definitely the main event and Stewarton was kept so busy he only had time to acknowledge me from across the room before I gave my talk.

Agnes, Lisa and Matt were in the audience and cheered when I'd finished. For most of the day we all stuck together even though I encouraged them to mingle and network. To be fair, they all made useful contacts, but we were all looking forward to the festive ball.

'I'm wondering what this dress you've knitted looks like, Agnes,' said Matt.

'It's stunning,' Lisa told him.

'I always think of knitting as well...woolly jumpers and bobble hats,' he said. 'Though I should know better having been at the knitting bee when you're all making whatever it is you make. I've still got the jumpers from last Christmas. And I wear them.' He smiled at Agnes. 'What's Santa knitting me this year?'

'A pair of woolly knickers if you dare to bare your all tomorrow night in your kilt,' said Agnes.

He grimaced. 'I don't fancy those. They'd itch the danglers off me.'

'Is everything okay?' Stewarton said, walking straight into Matt's comment.

'Eh, yes,' said Matt. 'I was just being an arse and getting them handed to me by the ladies. They keep me in line.'

Stewarton smiled and then said, 'The dinner is due shortly if you'd all like to get changed into your evening wear.'

'Thanks for letting us know,' I said to him.

'Sorry I haven't had a chance to talk to you. It's been a busy day.'

'That's okay,' I told him. 'We've enjoyed ourselves.'

Agnes looked out the windows. 'Is that more snow?'

Flurries of thick flakes fluttered past the windows.

'We'd better get our things from the cars,' I suggested.

Again, Stewarton insisted on bringing mine in even though Matt offered to get them. Both Stewarton and Matt told us to wait in the warmth of the mansion while they ventured outside and brought the bags in.

'I'm liking Stewarton more and more,' Agnes said wistfully as we watched the two figures in the snow.

Me too, I thought, feeling a longing I hadn't felt in a long time. Me too.

Agnes gave us a twirl. Her dress was gorgeous. She described the colour as vintage cream.

'It looks as if you've knitted yourself a soft lace dress,' said Matt. 'It doesn't look knitted, not in the sense I thought. What a stoater you look in it.'

Agnes smoothed her hands down the knitted bodice that draped down to a flowing gown that did indeed look like parts of it were made of lace.

'It's beautiful work, Agnes.' I admired every little detail she'd added. 'It's a perfect fit.'

'A flattering fit,' she said. 'I wanted something that made me a walking advert for my shop, so what better way than to wear a knitted evening dress. I just didn't anticipate it would do wonders for my figure.'

'The colour is so classy,' said Lisa.

'And you look lovely,' I said. 'What a job you've made of your dress. It is amazing.' I loved it. Sewn from satin and silk, it combined various shades of pale pink.

Lisa beamed with pride. 'I'm happy with it now. Seeing it in my living room it seemed a wee bit ostentatious, but in this setting, under the lights and with everyone dressed up to impress, I think it works. I was worried I'd outshine the Christmas tree but the tree has me beat on sparkle hands down.'

'I think we all look like we belong in this glamorous ball,' said Matt. He wore a dinner suit and had smoothed his hair back.

'And look at you in that ball gown sensation,' Agnes said to me.

'Some of the dresses in Delphine's shop are complete steals,' I said, swishing the chiffon and silk dress, enjoying being all dressed up, even if it was only for one night. I'd been to dinner dances before, but not an actual ball where most of the ladies wore proper ball gowns and the men wore classic dinner suits.

We headed into the hub of the ball. The meal the previous night had been great but an even more lavish menu was served for the festive ball.

We ate our dinner and chatted, and I kept looking at the scene — the twinkling lights, everything gleaming silver and gold, the traditional setting and decor that made me feel as if I was in one of those glamorous scenes from a film.

I hadn't seen Stewarton, but Ewan had swept past our table a couple of times. Finally he asked me to dance with him when we'd finished our dinner.

I let him lead me on to the dance floor which was quite busy with couples.

'You look beautiful in that dress, Tilsie,' he whispered in my ear as he pulled me close to waltz around the room.

I stepped on his toes a few times, but as my dress was full–length no one saw that my footwork wasn't up to par with most of the others. I hadn't deliberately stepped on his toes or kicked his shins as Agnes had suggested recently. I wasn't angry with Ewan any more. Had I forgiven him completely? I wasn't sure.

'Am I forgiven?' he said, as if reading my mind.

I pulled my head back as we continued to dance and looked up at him.

'You had those frown lines on your brow that you have when you're thinking deep thoughts,' he said. 'I assumed I was partly to blame for those.'

He'd guessed right.

'If you think you know me so well, then you really shouldn't be dancing with me. You should be dancing with someone else. There are lots of ladies here who would be delighted to enjoy your company I'm sure.' Definitely in his white jacket dinner suit that screamed class and money.

'Ah, we're back to the marriage thing.'

'No, it's just that —'

'It's okay, Tilsie,' he said, gazing down at me as the music slowed and the waltz steps became easier for me. 'I've been thinking deep thoughts too while I was away.'

'You're teasing me.'

'No, I may have to admit it's time I thought about settling down. Perhaps not this year, or next year, but maybe I am the marrying sort after all.'

There was nothing in his tone that convinced me he meant it. And even if he had reconsidered his views on marriage, I didn't feel close to him, especially when dancing. I remembered Agnes' advice that I would know when I danced with a man whether he was the one for me.

'You've got those frown lines again,' he said, smiling. 'What's up now?'

'Someone gave me advice. A real friend. And she was right.'

It was his turn to frown.

'I have forgiven you, Ewan, but I just don't want to get involved with you, even with the wispy mention of marriage somewhere on the horizon, one day, maybe never.'

'You're the first woman who has made me even consider marriage.' He sounded as if he blamed me, as if it was my fault he'd altered his views on tying the knot.

I stopped dancing and calmly pulled away from him. I began to walk off the dance floor, trying not to make a scene. I tried to look as if I'd finished dancing and wanted to take a break.

Matt was up dancing with Lisa, and as I headed back to my table, I saw a good–looking man of similar age to Agnes, deep in conversation with her. I doubted they were talking shop. He was flirting with her. Chatting her up. So I headed over to admire the Christmas tree adorned with baubles and lights that definitely outshone even Lisa's ball gown.

Ewan followed me. 'Come and sit with me at my table.'

'No, you go back. I'm taking a breather over here.'

I gazed out at the snow scene trying to let the sparkling white scenery calm my senses.

Minutes later, two elegant hands appeared over my shoulders. 'I thought you might need this.' Stewarton placed my silver and white wrap around me.

I hugged it close to me even though the room was warm. I welcomed the comfort of my knitted wrap and of Stewarton.

'Thank you, Stewarton.'

'Excuse me, Sir,' a member of staff interrupted us. 'There's an urgent call for you in reception. I think it has something to do with tomorrow night's céilidh.'

The muscles in Stewarton's finely–sculptured jaw tightened. Bad timing for him again. He excused himself and left me to watch him go. I hugged the wrap around my arms and wondered what would've happened if we hadn't been interrupted. Would he have said things to me that deep down I wanted to hear? Would I have done what Ewan did and changed my mind about my plans when it came to romance?

I gazed out at the snowy night and wondered if I'd made the right choice this winter to put romance on ice.

I didn't see Stewarton again that night. Matt said he'd seen Ewan leave the ball early. We left at a reasonable time, having danced together and enjoyed the ball and the fantastic dinner.

I decided to keep my dress on to drive home, but wore my boots and the cosy wrap. It was after midnight when I drove through the snow wearing the loveliest dress I'd ever worn. This dress was a keeper. So too were the dear friends I'd made in Agnes, Lisa and loveable Matt. As for Ewan and Stewarton, I wondered what would happen with them. Would any feelings I harboured for Stewarton melt with the snow?

Unsure what to do, I decided to take the safe option and protect my heart from being broken by yet another handsome and charming man. At least for now. For the festive season. Christmas snuggled up in front of the television on my own didn't seem so bad. In my heart, I welcomed the relaxation. It had been a busy year for my marketing business. I'd made a substantial profit, though I'd worked hard for it. There were still four manic weeks on the run up to Christmas Day and plenty of work to be done. That's what I'd do, I told myself firmly. Concentrate on work and let romance drift along with the snow.

Then my heart jolted when I remembered. I still had to go to the conference on Sunday. And the céilidh. I almost wished that Matt would go commando under his kilt. That would surely be memories for the archives, to think back on when the conference was finished, and I had no more reason to be in touch with Stewarton.

My talk on the Sunday was rescheduled, again due to people not arriving on time. I was on first, so I gave my talk and then decided to drive back into the city rather than hang around the conference all day. The céilidh wasn't until 8:00 p.m. with a supper midway through the evening at around 9:30 p.m.

That evening, I put my dress on, the one the ladies had helped make for me, the one with the little Christmas tree patterned fabric. I loved the vintage ball gown, but this dress was extra special. I'd never seen anything like it and as they'd made it from scratch for me it had a custom fit. It felt so comfortable, from the short cap sleeves to the heart–shaped neckline, fitted waist and long flowing skirt. The skirt was manageable. One of the ladies, the seamstress, adjusted the pattern, taking the width of the hemline in so it would be easier for Scottish dancing. The women had also advised me to wear the proper dancing shoes that were both comfy and suitable for my dress.

The night was freezing and I wore my wrap as I parked outside the knitting shop and hurried in. I'd phoned and agreed to meet Agnes and the others at the shop. Matt said he'd drive us all there and back, and I was looking forward to having a laugh with them.

Agnes was giving Matt a friendly telling off when I arrived. He'd given her a burl to show off his kilt and she got an eyeful of what was under it.

'You're not escorting us to the céilidh with your macaroons on show,' she told him.

'My kilt's down to my knees,' he said, smiling at her. 'You can't see anything. It's only when I do this...' He gave another twirl.

'Cover those up,' she scolded him.

All he did was laugh. Lisa and I smiled at each other.

Agnes marched over to her cupboard and rummaged through the piles of knitting. 'I warned you, Matt. I warned you.' She threw a pair of soft wool underpants at him. 'Put these on.'

122

'Woolly pants?' he said, holding them at arm's length. Then his hands felt the fabric. 'These are soft as butter.'

We all looked away as Matt pulled them on. He walked up and down the shop. 'These feel very nice, Agnes. I think I'll keep them on.'

'You'd better keep them on, Matt, or you'll get a hiding from me,' she said.

'We've time for a quick cup of tea before we go,' said Lisa, sorting the cups up while the kettle boiled.

'It'll heat us up before we head out,' said Agnes. 'I think it's going to be an exciting night. I can feel the excitement in my bones, and I'm never wrong about these things.'

While we drank our tea, I tried not to dwell on thoughts of Stewarton and that this was the last night of the conference.

Every time I thought about Stewarton my heart ached a little, and I pushed him aside to try and concentrate on the céilidh dancing. Although Matt had promised to teach me a few steps for the main dances, we hadn't done it. But never one to let things like that bother him, he offered to teach me in the shop.

'When you twirl around, turn under my arm and then skip to the left,' he instructed.

I gave it a go and almost knocked Agnes' mannequin into Santa's grotto. I swear I heard his squeaker give a frightened beep.

'There's no room in here to learn how to do a Scottish reel,' I told him. 'I'll just have to wing it when we get there.'

Matt looked outside at the snow–covered street. It hadn't snowed all day, but the freeze held strong and the pavement glittered as if encrusted with diamante. Then he looked at my boots. I'd kept my shoes in a bag.

Matt, wearing full Highland dress and a kilt with more swing in it than any man had a right to have, grabbed me by the hand and pulled me outside.

'No, Matt, no,' I squealed while Agnes and Lisa laughed.

'Just one wee go,' he said. 'You can get a heat in the car in a couple of minutes. You'll not freeze if you're dancing. Now come on, twirl under my arm, skip to the left and then repeat that to the right.

So I gave it a go. I danced for a few minutes in the snowy street with Matt. Two fools creating merry hell. All Agnes and Lisa did was howl with laughter — until Ewan appeared from his shop, locking up for the night. He was dressed in a dark kilt and fitted velvet jacket. He looked good, but Matt suited his kilt better.

Ewan's expression was as cold as the night air. 'What are you idiots up to? Dancing in the ruddy snow.' The tone of disapproval in his voice rang clear in the icy stillness, perhaps mixed with a hint of jealousy that I was happy to dance with Matt even under these crazy circumstances.

Matt beat me to a response, and after hearing what he said, I felt no need to add anything.

Matt glared over at Ewan and shouted, 'Take your rotten attitude, Ewan, stick it up your kilt and light it.'

And then we all drove off to the céilidh.

Agnes wore a long burgundy velvet skirt with a white blouse and silk tartan waistcoat. Lisa wore a similar outfit only her skirt was bottle green velvet.

The dance floor was jumping with activity when we arrived and everyone was dressed in their finery.

'I think Ewan's got a burr up his bahookie tonight,' Matt said, watching Ewan strutting past without looking at us.

'He'll have the toe of my nice shoes up it if he gives us the snub again.' Agnes' voice carried over the crowd and I saw Ewan's shoulders jolt when he heard her. He kept walking and didn't glance back at us.

Lisa pursed her lips and then said, 'I think he's jealous.'

'That my kilt's bigger than his?' Matt joked.

'You certainly look better in a kilt than he does, which is surprising as he's a real looker,' said Lisa.

Matt blinked. 'Was there a compliment in there somewhere?'

Lisa smiled and continued. 'He's acting like a man who fancies someone.' She looked straight at me. 'And the lady in question isn't interested in him. I bet that's a new experience for Ewan.'

'Well, let's not bother with Ewan,' I said. 'I've a whole evening ahead of embarrassing myself on the dance floor.'

'Were you thinking of doing something outrageous?' said Stewarton as he approached us. He was wearing his kilt and traditional shirt and jacket. 'Not that I would complain if you did.'

The music turned up a notch and everyone got ready to do one of the fast–moving reels. I was pulled on to the floor whether I was ready or not. Mainly I was not.

Stewarton held one hand and Matt held the other as we prepared to whirl around dancing one of the fastest reels of the night.

'I don't know how to do these dances,' I warned Stewarton.

Stewarton tried not to laugh.

'Laugh if you want,' I told him. 'I'm just giving you warning to keep your toes out of my way and pretend you don't know me if I embarrass you horribly.'

'You could never do that,' he called to me as the reel started to pick up pace.

'Don't count on it,' I called back to him, and then held on for dear life as the pace got faster and faster.

Screams of glee, howls and hoots of joy, descanted with the live music. And suddenly it didn't matter that I didn't know the steps. I was caught up in the sheer fun and excitement. I'd never felt such energy in a room full of people in my whole life. I knew I'd never forget it.

And I'd never forget dancing with Stewarton. Something in me changed when we danced together. He wasn't the best dancer, but he knew all the steps and was fit and strong enough to hurl me around the room. Sometimes I was partnered with Matt, then I linked arms and danced parts of the reel with Agnes and Lisa, and others. Then I was back holding tight to Stewarton as he danced my socks off.

By the time we'd finished, which was a while, because as one dance finished another merged and we continued to whirl around the dance floor, my face was sore from laughing and smiling. My feet were fine. The shoes were great for dancing in as was my dress.

'Is it okay if we sit this one out?' I said to Stewarton as I flopped down on a chair near the log fire they'd lit specially for the céilidh.

Matt, Agnes and Lisa were still going strong, dancing and having a great time.

'Fine by me.' Stewarton sat on the opposite side of the fire. 'Just a cosy night relaxing by the fire,' he joked.

The hurly–burly of the céilidh swirled around us, and outside the snow was falling fast. And yet I enjoyed a moment of calm, a tiny pocket of time with Stewarton, pretending we were relaxing by the fireside.

'It's been quite a weekend,' I said. 'By your standards, was the conference a success?'

'A roaring success, and thanks to you for being one of the speakers. We had an interesting mix this year. It worked well.'

'And now what? Do you go back to your normal business? Or have you other events planned?'

'Nothing planned. This is a yearly event, so that's it until next November. Maybe I could pencil you in for a second year?'

'If we're still in touch.'

A sadness crossed his face. 'I hope we will be. Perhaps I can find an excuse to keep in touch with you every now and again, though that's how people drift, isn't it?'

I nodded. 'Such is life.'

'Indeed, but I'll certainly remember this weekend for a long time.'

'Me too.'

'Will you be taking time off from your hectic schedule to enjoy Christmas?' he said.

'That's the plan. Snuggling down, cooking myself Christmas dinner and watching the television while eating far too much chocolate.'

'I did enjoy our evening at the chocolatier's shop. Maybe another time, when things are more settled in your life.'

Again, he was trying to get the timing right and yet...there we were saying our goodbyes.

'Maybe.' Something inside me was yelling that I should take a chance with him, but I didn't. I couldn't do it. I think he sensed this.

'Would you like a drink? A mulled wine?' he offered.

'That would be lovely.'

He got up and went to get our drinks, leaving me sitting by the fire. He'd only been gone a few moments when Ewan approached. My heart sank. This was not going to end well.

Chapter Fifteen

The Knitting Bee

Ewan swaggered over and sat down beside me. He draped his arm around the back of my chair, possessive, determined to flirt with me.

'You're the loveliest woman here,' he said, giving me the full impact of his stunning blue eyes. 'Come home with me tonight. We can make things work. Give me a chance. Every man deserves a second chance.'

'You've been drinking.'

He shook his head adamantly. 'One small whisky toast when I arrived. Nothing more than that.'

'I can smell it on your breath.'

He continued his arrogant tone. 'Must be the sherry trifle.'

He leaned in to try and kiss me but I pulled away, and that's when Stewarton came back with our drinks.

Ewan didn't flinch and sneered up at him. 'Ah, thank you waiter. Just put them down on the table before you go.'

'Do you want me to go?' Stewarton asked me.

I stared wide–eyed at him, and in that second Ewan stood up and faced–off with Stewarton. They were a fair match for each other in height, but Ewan had Stewarton beat on arrogance.

Stewarton put the drinks down without stepping back. He wasn't prepared to give an inch.

I noticed a few people pausing to watch. The air felt tense as if a fight was a hair's trigger from kicking off.

'Leave now, Ewan.' Stewarton couldn't have made his message any clearer or colder.

'What? Leave the party? No way, the night's still young and I've dancing to do with Tilsie here. Isn't that right?' he said to me.

I sat where I was, fearing if I got up to leave it would be the spark needed to cause an actual fight.

'Go away, Ewan,' I said calmly. 'Just go before there's any trouble.'

Ewan smirked at me. 'Trouble? What trouble would there be, unless your boyfriend here wants to start it?'

I saw Matt and the girls heading our way. Matt had a determined expression and pushed through the crowded dance floor to reach us. But he was too late. Ewan took Stewarton unawares and threw a sneaky punch at him, skimming his knuckles against his jaw. The fighter in Stewarton ducked to avoid being hit and only minor contact was made.

I thought that someone had alerted security, and saw the surprise on people's faces that a real fight was brewing amid the party atmosphere.

'There will be no trouble in here tonight, Ewan.' Stewarton's voice rang clear above the music and chatter.

Ewan gave him a triumphant sneer. 'No, I didn't think there would be.' Ewan was a strong, fit, man and looked like he'd be a hard man to beat in a fight.

A lull fell over the party revelry as Stewarton said, 'So get the hell outside and we'll finish it there.'

Well, I tried to stop them. I did. I really did. But there was nothing I could do. While the dancing continued and the band played on, Stewarton opened one of the patio doors and stepped outside into the snowy night.

The freezing cold air poured in but was soon warmed by the heat of the party. Those who noticed a fight was about to kick off, came to watch, but most people never even knew that the conference host was about to hammer hell out of one of the guests.

He was, wasn't he? Ewan was in for a surprise. There was nothing in his boastful manner to indicate he knew that Stewarton, just as tall but of a lighter build, could give him a tanking.

'Do you want me to try and stop them?' Matt said to me.

'I don't know.' I turned to Agnes and Lisa. 'Is security coming to deal with this?' I certainly didn't want Matt to get hurt and I'd seen fights before when it was the man who tried to separate them who got the brunt of it.

By now Stewarton had led Ewan on to the snow–covered lawn. In parts, the snow reached above their ankles, but the traditional, thick cream woollen socks they wore with their kilts kept out the chill.

'You really like her so much, huh, that you're prepared to fight for her?' Ewan sounded incredulous, but he was also baiting his rival.

Stewarton didn't take the bait, but his reply took my breath away.

'I'll always fight for her. I'll fight for her to the bitter end.'

Agnes gripped my arm and we exchanged a look.

That's when I decided to stop things escalating any further, but now it was my timing that was out. I was too late. Ewan lunged at Stewarton, intent on smashing his fist into his face.

The fight that followed was fast and furious. Ewan didn't stand a chance though he tried to give a good account of himself.

Their kilts, jackets and hair were covered in snow and their bare knuckles looked raw–boned freezing.

'Don't get up again, Ewan,' Stewarton shouted down at him, 'or I'll knock your bloody lights out.'

Ewan tried a dirty trick. He tried to kick Stewarton in the shins, but his opponent was wise to that move and instead punched him on the jaw, sending him flying back on to the snow.

A cheer from the unofficial crowd went up. I guessed Ewan wasn't as popular as I thought he was.

Security lifted Ewan up, dusted him down and helped him away.

'Make sure he gets attended to properly and taken home,' said Stewarton, brushing the snow from his kilt.

The crowd melted back into the party, and as the snow fell where the fight had been, all traces were sprinkled with fresh snow in minutes, as if the skirmish had never happened.

Matt and the girls tactfully gave Stewarton a private moment to talk to me before we went back inside. We were alone long enough for him to apologise for what had happened.

'I'm sorry you had to see that, Tilsie.'

'Are you hurt?'

He shook his head. 'And I tried not to do Ewan an injury. I reckon in the morning only his pride will hurt.'

'And his jaw. That was quite a punch you gave him.'

He didn't look proud of himself. There was no winner's swagger from him, though I knew if Ewan had been the winner he'd have lauded it over everyone.

'Excuse me, Stewarton, said a member of staff, once again cutting short our conversation. 'Security need to talk to you. Ewan insists on driving himself home. No one wants to involve the police but he's in no state to drive.'

'I'll be right there. Ask Alec to handle things until I get there.'

The man hurried away.

As the snow sprinkled down around us, we both knew it was time to part.

'My parents are spending Christmas in New York. They often go away for the holidays. Sometimes I join them, but this year I want them to have time to themselves so I've booked a cottage further north.' He told me the location. 'So if you're ever passing during the Christmas and New Year break, you're welcome to drop by for an eggnog.' I think he was intending keeping the conversation light.

I smiled at him. 'That's almost a hundred miles from here. I won't be passing near there any time soon.'

He shrugged. 'I thought it polite to make the offer.'

'Have a great Christmas,' I said.

'And you.'

I thought for a moment he was going to kiss me. I hesitated and so did he.

'Stewarton? Can you please come and deal with Ewan?' the staff member called.

Stewarton smiled at me one last time and then he was gone. I didn't see him again that night, though the céilidh was already starting to wind down.

Matt drove us back to Agnes' shop.

'Come in for a tea before you drive home,' Agnes said to me.

We all went inside and Agnes flicked the Christmas tree lights on and we sat in the shop discussing the events of the night and drinking our tea.

'I didn't know Stewarton could fight like that,' said Matt.

'He trained as a fighter years ago along with Caelan Broadie the chocolatier.' I filled him in on the details.

'I always quite fancied doing a bit of boxing myself,' said Matt.

'It wouldn't have suited you,' Agnes told him. 'You've got too easy–going a nature. I think you've got to have a wild streak in you to be a great fighter.'

Matt's chest expanded. 'Was that a compliment, Agnes? Are you saying I'm a nice fella after all?'

'Don't push your luck, Matt, or Santa might forget to leave you a present this year,' she said.

'What am I getting?' he asked.

'It's a surprise,' said Agnes.

'Is it a jumper? I wouldn't say no to another jumper.'

She shook her head as he continued to try and guess what she'd knitted for him.

Lisa whispered to me. 'It's a couple of smart waistcoats. One of them is knitted in seed stitch and backed with gents satin from the tailor's shop.'

'What was that?' said Matt.

'I was just mentioning about Stewarton's kilt,' said Lisa.

Agnes nodded. 'His kilt has as much swing in it as yours, Matt. When he was out in the snow fighting, I didn't know where to look when he spun round to defend himself and then spun back again.'

'I think you knew fine where to look,' said Lisa. 'What an eyeful.' She looked at me and smiled. 'Did you see him?'

I had noticed. It was difficult not to. I nodded.

Agnes laughed. 'Oh my goodness, there's a Christmas present for you, Tilsie.'

'Agnes!' I said.

'Oh, so it's okay for Stewarton to display his swingers, but I've got to wear a pair of woollies to hide mine,' said Matt. 'Speaking of knickers, I'd better give you these back.' He went to take his woolly undies off but we all screamed at him in unison.

'No,' said Agnes. 'Keep them. They're yours.'

'Thanks, Agnes. They were very comfy. And eh, can I ask how things went with that businessman who was chatting you up at the table while Lisa and I were dancing? He seemed to fancy his chances.'

'I'm doing what Tilsie is doing — keeping my options open and not getting involved too easily. Men are often nothing but trouble. Present company accepted.'

Having finished our tea, shared more gossip and gasps about what we saw under quite a few kilts, I drove home.

The weekend was one I kept thinking about as the weeks flew by to Christmas. The more time passed, the more I convinced myself I'd done the right thing regarding Stewarton. Though sometimes, in my dreams, I saw him fight for me in the snow and remembered what he'd said — 'I'll always fight for her.'

I kept myself busy with work, with knitting and with baking. I baked my Christmas cake — a light fruit sponge with buttercream and loads of sprinkles. I cooked pots of soup and froze it so I had plenty of meals in the freezer. Although I intended cooking a traditional Christmas dinner with all the trimmings, it was handy to have things like lentil soup and broth in the freezer to heat up after a busy day.

At the last Wednesday night knitting bee before the holidays we had our Christmas Knitting Bee party at the shop. Everyone baked and brought cakes, mince pies and homemade ginger wine. I made fairy cakes with silver baubles on them.

Agnes' mannequin wore my céilidh dress to promote the Christmas tree fabric, but this brought up the subject of the céilidh and inevitably the conversation involved questions about Stewarton. The women had seen plenty of photographs of him from the pictures Agnes and Lisa took at the parties.

'What's happening with you and Stewarton?' one of the ladies asked me as we gossiped and enjoyed our tea, cakes and ginger wine.

'Nothing. He might invite me to speak again at the conference next year.'

There was a lull.

'Nothing?' the woman said. 'Don't you fancy him? He's luscious. If I was younger I'd snap him up.'

Several others agreed and before I knew it I was trying to explain why I didn't want to date Stewarton. Even I heard that my excuses sounded feeble.

One of the ladies frowned at me. 'So you'd rather have no romance in your life now than date a man you like and who loves you?'

Put like that my reasons sounded ridiculous.

Another member said, 'He seems such a presentable man. Single, well–off, a hard worker. And he is, as we've all agreed, *gorgeous*.'

Another lull.

'Tilsie's had difficult relationships with boyfriends in the past,' said Agnes. 'She's wary of getting involved.'

'But you could miss your chance at happiness,' one of them said. 'When it comes to love, you've got to take a chance. Nothing's guaranteed. If it was, we'd all be settled with our men and in happy relationships, but that's just not real life.'

'Julie was here this afternoon,' said Agnes.

'Julie?' Her name felt like a dagger through my chest.

'Yes, I was going to phone you but the shop got busy so I thought I'd tell you tonight.'

'What did she want?' I asked, hoping it wasn't Stewarton.

'She wanted information about Ewan,' Agnes explained. 'She wanted to know if he'd shut his shop for good today and planned to move into new premises on the other side of the city just after Christmas.'

This was news to me, though the others seemed to know that Ewan had shut up shop.

'So he's moved?' I said.

'Yes, to bigger premises yet again. He says it's got plenty of room for his stock,' said Agnes. 'So I told Julie that he'd moved.'

'What's it got to do with her?' I said. 'She's not thinking of moving into the vacant shop is she?'

'Noooo.' Agnes sounded relieved. 'She had her eye on the other premises, the one he's moved into. She wasn't pleased. She wanted that premises. She *wanted* it,' Agnes said, imitating Julie.

I think that hearing Julie's name was the thing that made me change my mind about things. About Stewarton.

'What time does Matt open his shop in the morning?' I asked Agnes.

'Early. He's always there very early. Why?'

At the crack of dawn I parked my car outside Matt's mountaineering shop. The shop was closed but he was inside sorting his stock. His Christmas tree in the front window was unusual. I'd never seen one that had crampons tied with tinsel on it or hiking boots stuffed with candy cane.

He smiled when he saw me and came hurrying to open the door. 'To what do I owe this pleasure?'

'It's Christmas Eve and I need to drive over a hundred miles north through the snow to this location.' I pulled out a scrap of paper printed with a map.

'Stewarton?'

I nodded. 'Yes.'

'Okay. Let's get you kitted out. You'll need thermals, proper boots, a weatherproof jacket...' He pointed to the changing room. 'Dive in there. I'll hand stuff in. When do you need to be there?'

'Now.' I threw my jacket and jumper off.

'Right. What transport are you planning?'

I popped my head out from behind the curtain. 'I'm taking the car.'

'Oh no, not that car.' He glanced at my car parked outside his shop.

'It's the only car I have. Do you think I should hire one?'

'No, you can borrow mine. I have two. Take my four–by–four. It can handle most terrain. The further north you drive the tougher the road will be with the snow. Keep in touch with me by phone and I'll keep you right along the way.'

I peered out at him again. 'Thanks, Matt.'

'Do you know how to put snow chains on the tyres?'

My heart lurched. 'Snow chains?'

'Never mind. I'll give you the short course on what to do.'

The drive was a total whiteout. How I ever got within shouting distance of Stewarton's cottage in the middle of nowhere was thanks to Matt's advice over the phone and sheer luck and determination.

It was dark by the time I'd run out of road, but at least I could see the lights from the cottage in the distance. Only one small field separated me from him. I could do this. I could. I shrugged my rucksack on to my back and ventured out.

I stumbled into ruts a few times and was covered head to toe in snow, but the front door to his cottage was in sight.

I hammered on the door, hoping he was in. He had to be in. The lights were on. It was the only cottage like this for miles and this was where he said he was staying.

The door opened and light flooded out. Stewarton stood there silhouetted against the warm glow of the cottage. 'Tilsie.'

'I was eh, passing by, and wondered if that eggnog was still on offer.'

He smiled at me, scooped me up in his arms and all but carried me inside. 'Eggnog and dinner.'

He helped me off with my rucksack and layers and layers of warm clothing.

'Matt kitted me out,' I said, as if this explained everything.

Stewarton sat me down beside the fire. He had a Christmas tree in the corner of the cottage and fairy lights sparkled on the branches. The glow from the fire flickered on the cream–painted walls and the colourful rugs gave a cosy atmosphere. The television was on but he'd muted the sound, probably wondering if he really did hear someone knocking on his door at night.

I wiggled my toes in front of the fire and unwound my scarf. I saw Stewarton busy in the kitchen. He was stirring a pot on the stove.

'Something smells delicious. I thought you couldn't cook.'

'I cheat. This is a heat it and eat it stew. There's plenty if you'd like some.'

'I'd love some. Can I give you a hand?'

He wandered through. 'No, it'll have to simmer for another few minutes.'

He stood there gazing at me. 'I can't believe you're here.'

'I changed my mind,' I said, gazing up at him.

I didn't have a chance to explain anything else because he leaned down, pulled me close to him and kissed me longingly, passionately.

I melted into him. 'I've missed you.'

He held me close and smiled. 'I've always missed you. I love you, Tilsie.'

'I love you too.'

Before the stew burned on the stove, he hurried into the kitchen to serve our dinner. He carried it through and put it on the table by the fire.

After the drive I'd had it tasted like the most delicious dinner in the world.

'I haven't finished knitting your Christmas present yet,' I told him. I went over to my rucksack and pulled out the bag containing his almost finished gift.

He gazed at me. 'You've knitted me a Christmas present?'

I nodded. 'I hope it fits. Jumpers are stretchy so it should.'

'A jumper?'

'I started it months ago, never knowing quite why, giving up sometimes and putting it aside to knit other things, but then I kept going back to it. As if somehow, I always knew or always hoped, this was for you, even though I wouldn't admit it to myself.'

'Can I see it?'

I opened the bag and pulled out the festive patterned jumper. It was a man's chunky knit sweater except I'd knitted a Christmas bauble design on the front. 'I unravelled it a few times. I wasn't sure what size of balls you'd like.'

He burst out laughing.

'Christmas balls,' I scolded him, giggling.

'I wasn't thinking of any other kind.'

'I have to finish off one of the cuffs and then I'm done, so if I started now I could have it ready to wrap and put under the tree for Christmas morning.'

He made a flourishing gesture, sat me down by the fire, put my feet up and handed me the knitting bag. 'I'll keep you supplied with tea and cake.'

'You have cake?'

'It's Christmas. Of course I have cake. And mince pies and goodness know what else. I arranged to have the cupboards stocked before I arrived. I often come up here when I want to get away from the city, away from it all.'

He made tea and gave me a slice of strawberry and cream sponge. He put it down on the coffee table and then sat down at the fireside with me.

He bit his lip.

'What's wrong?' I asked him.

'I haven't got a pressie for you.'

'Yes you have,' I told him.

The grey eyes viewed me and he smiled.

I looked around, at the cosy cottage, the Christmas tree, the fairy lights, and at him. 'This is the best Christmas present I could have wished for.' I relaxed back in my chair and started to knit the last few rows of his jumper, sipping my tea and eating cake.

He turned the television up and we watched a classic festive film.

'Just a cosy night in relaxing by the fire,' he said, reminding me of the evening at the céilidh.

I smiled at him. 'A cosy night in together.'

He leaned over and kissed me again. This time the timing was right.

End

About the Author:

Follow De-ann on Instagram @deann.black

De-ann Black is a bestselling author, scriptwriter and former newspaper journalist. She has over 80 books published. Romance, crime thrillers, espionage novels, action adventure. And children's books (non-fiction rocket science books and children's fiction). She became an Amazon All-Star author in 2014 and 2015.

She previously worked as a full-time newspaper journalist for several years. She had her own weekly columns in the press. This included being a motoring correspondent where she got to test drive cars every week for the press for three years.

Before being asked to work for the press, De-ann worked in magazine editorial writing everything from fashion features to social news. She was the marketing editor of a glossy magazine. She is also a professional artist and illustrator. Fabric design, dressmaking, sewing, knitting and fashion are part of her work.

Additionally, De-ann has always been interested in fitness, and was a fitness and bodybuilding champion, 100 metre runner and mountaineer. As a former N.A.B.B.A. Miss Scotland, she had a weekly fitness show on the radio that ran for over three years.

De-ann trained in Shukokai karate, boxing, kickboxing, Dayan Qigong and Jiu Jitsu. She is currently based in Scotland.
Her colouring books and embroidery design books are available in paperback. These include Floral Nature Embroidery Designs and Scottish Garden Embroidery Designs.

Also by De-ann Black (Romance, Action/Thrillers & Children's books). See her Amazon Author page or website for further details about her books, screenplays, illustrations, art and fabric designs.
www.De-annBlack.com

Romance books:

Sewing, Crafts & Quilting series:
1. The Sewing Bee
2. The Sewing Shop

Quilting Bee & Tea Shop series:
1. The Quilting Bee
2. The Tea Shop by the Sea

Heather Park: Regency Romance

Snow Bells Haven series:
1. Snow Bells Christmas
2. Snow Bells Wedding

Summer Sewing Bee
Christmas Cake Chateau

Cottages, Cakes & Crafts series:
1. The Flower Hunter's Cottage
2. The Sewing Bee by the Sea
3. The Beemaster's Cottage
4. The Chocolatier's Cottage
5. The Bookshop by the Seaside

Sewing, Knitting & Baking series:
1. The Tea Shop
2. The Sewing Bee & Afternoon Tea
3. The Christmas Knitting Bee
4. Champagne Chic Lemonade Money
5. The Vintage Sewing & Knitting Bee

The Tea Shop & Tearoom series:
1. The Christmas Tea Shop & Bakery
2. The Christmas Chocolatier
3. The Chocolate Cake Shop in New York at Christmas
4. The Bakery by the Seaside
5. Shed in the City

Tea Dress Shop series:
1. The Tea Dress Shop At Christmas
2. The Fairytale Tea Dress Shop In Edinburgh
3. The Vintage Tea Dress Shop In Summer

Christmas Romance series:
1. Christmas Romance in Paris.
2. Christmas Romance in Scotland.

Romance, Humour, Mischief series:
1. Oops! I'm the Paparazzi
2. Oops! I'm A Hollywood Agent
3. Oops! I'm A Secret Agent
4. Oops! I'm Up To Mischief

The Bitch-Proof Suit series:
1. The Bitch-Proof Suit
2. The Bitch-Proof Romance
3. The Bitch-Proof Bride

The Cure For Love
Dublin Girl
Why Are All The Good Guys Total Monsters?
I'm Holding Out For A Vampire Boyfriend

Action/Thriller books:
Love Him Forever
Someone Worse
Electric Shadows
The Strife Of Riley
Shadows Of Murder
Cast a Dark Shadow

Children's books:
Faeriefied
Secondhand Spooks
Poison-Wynd
Wormhole Wynd
Science Fashion
School For Aliens

Colouring books:
Flower Nature
Summer Garden
Spring Garden
Autumn Garden
Sea Dream
Festive Christmas
Christmas Garden
Christmas Theme
Flower Bee
Wild Garden
Faerie Garden Spring
Flower Hunter
Stargazer Space
Bee Garden
Scottish Garden Seasons

Embroidery Design books:
Floral Nature Embroidery Designs
Scottish Garden Embroidery Designs

Printed in Great Britain
by Amazon

83239417R00088